Graser10 and the Mysterious Castle: An Unofficial Adventure

By Graser10

ISBN-13: 978-1539600473
ISBN-10: 1539600475

Graser10 and the Mysterious Castle

G raser was excited. Everything was almost ready. His preparation looked as though it would all pay off. This would *definitely* be one to remember.

It was time to play Survival Challenge, one of Graser's all-time favorite games. When it came to creating fun competitions for his friends, few in the world of Minecraft could design them as well as Graser could.

This actually surprised some people. They tended to underestimate Graser. Especially if it was their first time meeting him. Mostly this was because Graser was a jet black robot with a big underbite, weird red eyes that glowed like magma, and blinking lights along his arms. Nobody knew what to expect from a robot like that, but they *certainly* didn't expect him to be one of the most talented crafters in the Overworld.

That was where most people were wrong.

Graser was renowned across the Overworld for his many innovative creations, and also for the knack he had for using what he'd crafted to win contests with his friends. In fact, Graser was *so* popular that thousands of people from across the Overworld came to watch his antics each week. Graser had crafted a palace for himself, in a style that befit a jet black robot with an underbite, and people came to the palace grounds. The palace itself was crafted from obsidian and coal and even some nether brick. The towers had lots of cool circular turrets. Graser's palace was one of the true wonders of the Overworld. Many rich and successful Minecrafters had

3

offered—or downright begged—to buy it from Graser over the years, but he would never sell. It was especially coveted by the zombies and skeletons in the neighborhood, who were always trying—unsuccessfully— to break in. The palace was perhaps his finest crafting achievement. Another feature that made the palace invaluable were the crafting grounds in front of it. The biome immediately surrounding the palace was a strange mix. There were mountains, ice spikes, fields of taiga, and even a desert-like area with spiny green cacti. From this strange mix of landscape features, Graser always seemed able to dig up whatever he needed. No matter how rare or obscure, Graser was always able to find what he needed somewhere in the area.

Whenever Graser did a crafting demonstration—as he was preparing to do today—people came from miles around to watch. Sometimes this meant that the big crowds trampled things, but Graser didn't care. He was happy to have an audience, and loved sharing crafting techniques with as many people as he could.

Today's Survival Challenge contest was going to be a doozy. Graser also thought it was one of his best ideas yet. Graser had constructed three enormous rectangles— each easily fifty feet high—out of gold and chiseled sandstone. They looked very much like giant picture frames. As Graser waited for his friends who would compete in the Survival Challenge, the crowd of onlookers gathered. Then, Graser's friends Will and Stacy showed up. They were famous crafters just like him, and would be competing in the challenge.

"Hi guys," Graser said enthusiastically. "Nice crowd we've got today, huh?"

Graser made a wide sweep with his black, robotic arm to indicate the curious onlookers.

"Cut to the chase," Will said cynically. "What insidious task have you got in mind for us? And, moreover, what are these giant gold squares?"

"I think they're actually rectangles," Stacy observed. "The sides are a bit taller than the horizontal parts."

"Rectangles, whatever," said Will. "What are you planning here, Graser?"

"The rules are simple," Graser said. "Today we're going to be painting self-portraits. With blocks. And they're going to be *enormous*."

"Huh?" Will and Stacy said, more or less in unison.

"Do I have to dumb it down?" Graser asked with a big smile. "You use blocks to make a big statue of your own faces inside one of the picture frames. We all have just twenty minutes to do it."

"I see," Will said cautiously. "And how do we decide who wins?"

"The audience will decide which portrait looks the best," Graser declared. "We'll have them vote by applause."

"I like it!" said Stacy.

"That's because *your* skin is the exact shade of sandstone, and there's a *ton* of sandstone around here," said Will. "It'll be easy for you!"

"Okay," said Graser. "No more talking. I'm already bored. And nobody likes a bored robot. Let's do this. One. . . two. . . three. . . GO!"

And with that, the latest Survival Challenge was underway!

All three of the contestants started mining for blocks that would let them form giant versions of themselves. Graser took out a diamond pickaxe and started mining for the darkest blocks he could find. Most of him managed to be a shade somewhere between coal and obsidian, so he concentrated on those two. Soon, a giant black robotic head began to fill the gold frame that Graser had selected for himself. The mouth and nose were no problem, but when it came to the eyes Graser took an entirely different approach. Graser mined for redstone, and then combined the stones into redstone blocks. When he had enough, he placed them in the center of the statue's eye sockets. However, he was sure to leave a little space between them. After the eyes were crafted, he crawled into the giant head and placed torches behind them. (It was a strange feeling to crawl inside of your own head, but Graser tried not to think about it too hard. He was usually good at doing that.) When he'd finished positioning the torches, they let out an eerie glow from behind the redstone. It was very much like Graser's own oil-fueled eyes. When that was completed, Graser had only to finish off the top of his head. He added a couple of diamond and emerald blocks to mimic the strange glowing buttons that popped up in strange places on his body.

No sooner had Graser put the final diamond block in place, than the timer he had set began to ring.

Graser took a few robotic steps back and paused to admire his creation.

"Dang it," said Will. "Graser's statue looks awesome."

"Yeah," agreed Stacy. "It's so realistic, I'm ready for it to open up its mouth and say something really stupid."

Graser glanced over at the virtual Minecraft portraits that Will and Stacy had created. They were also really, really good. Will and Stacy were both master-crafters. Still, their likenesses didn't have awesome glowing red eyes. Which, in Graser's opinion, left a lot to be desired.

"Let's see what our audience thinks," Graser said, turning to face the surrounding crowd. "Who likes Will's portrait the best?"

There was a polite golf-clap from a few people.

"I don't need your charity," Will said dourly.

"Okay," Graser said to the audience. "Now how about Stacy. I think she did a great job!"

A bit more polite applause. It was clear that most folks were saving their approval for Graser's creation. There was a palpable stillness in the air, like the calm before a wild storm.

"All right then," Graser said. "And who liked *my* portrait of-"

He was not even able to finish the sentence. The raucous roar of the crowd cut him off quite completely. People hooted and clapped their hands raw. There was no question as to who had won the Survival Challenge.

"Dang," said Will.

"You win again, Graser," said Stacy.

Graser only smiled graciously as the applause died down. Years of many awesome crafting successes had taught him to be gracious in victory. Or at least not to rub it in *too* much.

Satisfied that today's action was over, the audience began to depart. Will and Stacy prepared to leave for their home server planes too.

"Are you just going to leave these giant heads here?" Stacy asked.

"We could smash them?" suggested Will. "That might be fun."

"Would you want to smash your own head, or someone else's?" Stacy wondered.

"Um. . . I think you know that we both want to smash Graser's," Will replied.

The two crafters looked at one another and exchanged grins. Then they took out glistening diamond pickaxes.

"Fine," said Graser, "but I bet I can smash both of your statues before you can smash mine!"

And just like that, another game was afoot! Graser lived for playing games and devising new ones. Some games involved a lot of setup and planning. The more complicated and intricate the rules—and the more types of crafting the game involved—the better! But other times, games could be fun when they were the *least* complicated they possibly could be. Like who could smash something apart the fastest.

Graser took out his own diamond pickaxe and got to work. However, it was clear that Will and Sarah had a head start on him. Nonetheless, Graser did his best, smashing away!

"Ow!" cried Will as he smashed the inside of the Graser-statue's head. "These torches behind your eyes are hot!"

"Hey, they gave it the right look," Graser called back as his pickaxe made quick work of the statue of Will's face.

"What's with that glow anyway?" asked Stacy. "Can you tell me more about it?"

"*Stacy*!" Will shot back. "Never ask a robot about its glowing eyes. That's private, robot stuff."

Graser laughed.

"It's okay," Graser said. "I don't mind talking about it. I think my eyes burn oil. Mostly, that's what I run on. But it could also be magma or lava or something. You never know."

"Haven't you ever tried touching it?" Stacy pressed. "You know, to find out?"

"Touching my glowing eyes?" Graser said. "I'd *never* do that. I'd burn my fingers!"

"But didn't anybody ever tell you what you were made of, like when you were growing up?" Stacy asked.

Will lowered his pickaxe and put his hand over his face. Then he shook his head.

"What?" Stacy said, looking back and forth between Will and Graser.

"You always have a way of asking about the most inappropriate topic," Will said.

"Huh?" said Stacy. "Shut up. No I don't."

Graser laughed again.

"Robots are created," explained Graser. "We don't really have traditional families. And in terms of 'growing up'—once I was created, I was already 'up.' I've always been exactly like you see me today."

"But all robots get created, or built, or whatever," Stacy pointed out. "Don't you remember who created you?"

Graser shook his head no.

"That's been a big mystery my entire life," Graser said. "I just suddenly. . . *was.* I don't have any memory of where I actually came from. It was never explained to me."

"But aren't you curious?" Stacy pressed. "Don't you ever think about trying to find it out?"

Graser shrugged.

"Sometimes I wonder where I came from," Graser told her. "I know I must have had a creator. But I don't know how I would find out. I've never met anybody who seemed to know where robots like me come from."

"Oh," said Stacy. "Well if I ever hear anything about someone who creates robots, you'll be the first person I tell."

"Okay," said Graser. "That sounds good to me."

"Incidentally, you just lost," called Will. He was standing amidst the smashed-up ruins of what had once been a statue of Graser's head.

"Ehh, you win some you lose some," Graser said. "Besides, it was two against one. The important point is that everybody had fun."

Will and Stacy helped Graser clean up the debris that the Survival Challenge had left on the front of his property, then departed for their own server planes. Graser knew he would see them again soon for another fun crafting challenge of one form or another. He couldn't wait!

Graser returned to his palace, changed into his favorite pair of diamond boots (he had several), and fixed himself a delicious dinner of hot oil soup. After his filling meal, Graser felt tired after his long day of crafting, and retired to his bedroom. Graser's bed was like other beds in Minecraft, except that it had been finished with a layer of rock-hard stone bricks—which was absolutely perfect if you had a metal back. Graser spread himself out over his pleasantly rigid bed and began to dream.

Often, ideas for new crafting creations came to Graser while he slept. He didn't know exactly why this was, but it was very common for him to awaken with an exciting idea for a new structure to build. Graser often wondered why he slept at all. Did robots *need* to sleep, or had his creator simply programmed him to do this so he'd feel a bit more human? Graser never knew the answer.

Tonight however, something strange happened. Graser did not sleep well. He tossed and turned. Many times, it seemed to him that he heard noises outside his palace. (This was probably just his metal ears playing tricks, he assured himself. All of the local mobs had the sense to stay far away now. He hadn't had a zombie attack in months, and visits from skeletons were growing practically unheard of.)

When the first light of dawn began to creep over the horizon, Graser pulled himself out of bed. He wondered again why his mind was not able to rest. There seemed a strange electricity in the air.

Then he looked out the window, and saw it.

Graser's bedroom was in the tallest tower of his palace. The window gave him a clear view—not just of his palace grounds, but far across the biome beyond. And as Graser chanced to look out his window, he saw something very unusual. In the center of his grounds— very near to where yesterday's Survival Challenge had been held, there was a book. It was just sitting there, in the center of the crafting pit. It was square and brown, just like so many other books in Minecraft. But one thing set it apart. Scrawled across the cover in bright red letters was one word: GRASER. The letters were so large, Graser could read them even from the great height of his tower.

Graser narrowed his robot eyes.

This was very strange. He owned no book like that. (Graser kept all his own books downstairs in his library, and he would *never* think of scrawling his name across the covers.) How odd. Graser decided to investigate. He left his bedroom and made his way down the winding circular staircase below the tower. (Being a robot eliminated the need to shower and shave every morning, which Graser had always considered a great time-saving feature. He did sometimes take oil baths, but only before very special occasions.)

Graser left his palace and stalked straight to his crafting area. The book was still there. And it still said GRASER.

Graser looked around. His glowing eyes surveyed the surrounding hills and trees. Had someone left this here for him? Was this some kind of a prank? A joke? Graser had annoyed so many crafters over the years— sometimes by making stupid jokes, but mostly by being better at crafting than they were—that he had a pretty extensive list of enemies. Accordingly, he was always a little bit suspicious.

Graser prodded the book with his metal toe. Nothing exploded. No alarms went off. No angry creepers spilled out of the ground, angry and ready to detonate.

So far so good.

Graser took a deep breath and bent down. He picked up the book and turned it over in his hands. It felt normal. Right weight. Correct material. Graser began to feel it was not a prank after all. But then what was it?

Graser opened the book.

Inside was written a very short message. The letter began in a flowery, formal hand.

However, the content of the message was astounding to the young robot. It shook him to his molten core.

Graser,

You have reached the age when certain things will be revealed to you. You were created by a legendary crafter, and were the pinnacle of his art—the greatest thing he ever built. He knew this on the day he completed you, yet he also knew you were made for a great purpose.

You have lived long enough to prepare yourself. Now it is time for the truly important test of your metal. . . and your mettle.

Many miles to the east, across the Blue Ice Plains Spikes biome and across the Extreme Hills of Sledding, lies Redstone Castle. If you can complete the journey there and solve the castle's mysteries, you will pass the test. If you pass the test, you will then meet your creator, and all mysteries will be revealed.

That was all it said.

Graser looked around again, still wondering if this was some kind of a joke. Graser had never received a message like this. He hardly knew what to think! It was certainly appealing to imagine that he had been created by someone who was a legendary crafter. 'Legendary' sounded so serious and dramatic! And it was also appealing to believe he had been made to complete an important quest. (Most of the time, Graser seemed to have been created to craft things while making really stupid jokes. . . because that was basically what he did all day.)

Hmm, Graser thought to himself. Could this message actually be real?

Graser knew that there was indeed an Ice Plains Spikes biome far to the east from his palace. And the spikes of ice *were* a particular shade of blue there. But it was so far away that Graser had only make the trip once or twice. And he'd *never* ventured beyond it. Were there extreme hills beyond it? (Where, apparently, people sledded?) And a castle beyond *that*?

Graser didn't know. . . but he suddenly wanted very much to find out.

Graser decided to trust that the message in the book was real! It was a risk, but a risk he was willing to take. Many things about the message were strange. Not least, that someone had written it down . . .and then left it for him to find. If you had something to tell Graser, you could just knock on his palace door and tell him. Everybody was welcome to do that. . . except the local zombies and skeletons. (Technically, zombies and skeletons were more than welcome to do this, but they were also liable to get smacked with a diamond sword if they did.) Graser thought that maybe whoever had written the note had a good reason for delivering it this way. Maybe the author needed to hide himself—or herself—because they were somebody that Graser already knew. Maybe the author of the note was *the very person who had built Graser*!

This last thought was so exciting that Graser momentarily became lightheaded. (This, of course, was not literal, because Graser's head was made of metal and actually weighed quite a lot.) When he recovered, Graser committed himself to begin his quest without delay. He still had many questions about what was going on, but heading to Redstone Castle and dealing with these "mysteries" the note spoke of seemed like an excellent first step. Graser returned to his palace and began filling his inventory with everything he might need. He had the sense that a long, strange journey might lie just ahead.

Graser set out later that morning. He locked the door to his palace and headed east down the small dirt trail that led away across the Overworld. As he walked, Graser had the distinct feeling he might be forgetting something. This was not necessarily because there was anything *to* forget. The note had not said he needed to bring anything at all. Rather, Graser was always forgetting things. It would be unusual if he did remember everything he needed.

As he walked, Graser mentally reviewed his inventory. He was wearing his most comfortable and broken-in pair of diamond boots. He also had two backup pairs just in case he might need them. He'd brought a large supply of oil for eating, drinking, and applying directly to his joints if he started to squeak. He also brought his crafting tools and all of the crafting materials he used most often. Graser didn't know what problems he might encounter on his trip, but experience had showed him that almost any problem could be solved with solid crafting.

When he reached the crest of the first hill, Graser turned and took one look back behind him. The towers of his palace stretched high into the sky behind him. He wondered how long it would be before he saw them again.

Graser took a deep breath, turned his back to the palace, and continued on across the hillside.

The next biome to the east was a taiga. It had subtle hills here and there, but was mostly flat and filled with spruce trees and ferns. Along the edges of the spruce trees, Graser found he could sometimes make out tiny flickers of grey. He knew that these were wolves. Probably they were wondering if he would be good to eat, or just fun to mess with. Because he was made of metal, mobs like wolves were less interested in trying to make a meal out of Graser. However, that didn't mean he was entirely safe from them. Sometimes creatures attacked him just for fun. Mobs could be real jerks that way.

In the center of the taiga was a village. Villagers often built their villages close to where famous or important crafters lived. A big reason for this was that they could call on the crafters whenever they needed something. On the other hand, the villagers often brought presents for the famous crafters or gave them information they might find useful. It was a reciprocal relationship.

The path Graser followed led right through the center of the village. As he approached, a white-robed librarian villager stepped up to greet him.

"Graser!" said the librarian. "I watched you win the Survival Challenge yesterday! It was great fun! Those giant sculptures really did look like the crafters, especially yours."

"Aww shucks," said Graser. He was often humble when praised.

"What brings you this way?" asked the librarian.

"I'm going on a trip, and it might be a long one," Graser said. "Watch out for skeletons and zombies until I get back. I won't be around to keep you safe."

"Okay," said the librarian. "I don't know if that will be a problem. The skeletons and zombies haven't been giving us too much trouble lately. In fact, they've been mysteriously quiet. It's almost like they've decided to go somewhere. That's not a bad thing, though. That's a good thing."

"I agree with you," said Graser. "Maybe they finally got the message about not being jerks all the time."

"Yeah," agreed the librarian. "Even the wolves have been behaving themselves."

"That's good news too," Graser said. "Anyhow, take care until I get back. So long!"

"Bye, Graser," the librarian called as Graser stalked through the village and across the rest of the taiga.

On the other side of the taiga was a vast desert biome. It had sloping hills of brown sandstone punctuated by bright green shocks of cacti and sugar cane. Tiny gold rabbits played in the sand. They looked on curiously as Graser approached.

"This trip is going to get hotter before it gets cooler," Graser said to himself with a grin.

He entered the desert biome cautiously. Because he was made of heavy metal, Graser had a habit of sinking into the sand. This was less dangerous than it was annoying. When the sand got up to his knees, it could get into his joints. When that happened, the grains made a grating, grinding sound whenever Graser took a step. It made sneaking a distinct impossibility. Of all the types of biome, deserts were probably his least favorite.

Graser grit his metal teeth and picked up his pace. If he *had* to cross a desert, he would do so as quickly as he could.

The first half of the desert biome went past without incident. Graser avoided stumbling into any cacti, and even avoided getting sand in his gears. Everything seemed to be going swimmingly. Then Graser spied something on the horizon that felt out of place. It was a villager pulling a cart across a hill of sand. That wasn't so strange, but the way this one was pulling his cart was entirely wrong. Whereas most of the time pulling a cart meant it followed down the road after you, in this case the villager never seemed to do anywhere. And the cart seemed only to fall slightly deeper into the sandy hill where it stood.

Instantly, the situation became clear to Graser. He sprinted over.

"Omigosh," said the villager as Graser drew near. "Thank goodness someone has come along. Can you help?"

"That remains to be seen," Graser said. "I mean, I'll try."

"O thank you," said the villager. He was an old man who looked as though his best cart-pulling days were long behind him.

It was clear to Graser that the man's cart had gotten caught in a sandy sinkhole. There was not even anything inside the cart. Even so, it was submerging right into the sand.

"Why did you pull your cart up to this hill?" Graser asked as he inspected the problem. "There's a path that runs through with no sinkholes at all."

"I wanted to see the cacti on the other side of the hill," the old villager said. "My brother told me they look totally awesome. He was right!"

For the first time, Graser glanced at the cacti that grew past the sinking cart. The old man was right. They grew extra tall, and their arms were posed in cool-looking twists and turns, almost like they were human dancers.

"I see what you mean," Graser said.

"So, can you help me save my cart or what?" asked the old man.

"Let's try pushing together," said Graser.

Both the old man and the black robot stood behind the cart and pushed as hard as they could. They pushed so hard that Graser was afraid they might actually break the cart itself. Still, it did not move. The cart's round wooden wheels were almost entirely submerged in the sand. They would not turn at all.

"Oh no," said the elderly villager as he lay panting beside the cart. "It's not going to work. My cart will be stuck here forever. Soon, it'll get covered in so much blowing sand that I won't even be able to find it. Hmm.

Maybe that's how these other hills got here. Maybe they're all just carts that got covered in sand."

Graser thought this hypothesis was a little weird.

"Don't give up just yet," said Graser. "I've got an idea."

Graser reached into his inventory and took out a stick and six iron ingots. He began combining them using his crafting tools. The old villager looked on with great curiosity.

"What are you doing?" he asked. But soon it was obvious. Graser was building a rail. When it was finished, Graser used it to lay down a track in front of the cart that led all the way back to the main path.

"Gee, that could work," said the old man. "But how are we going to get my cart onto those rails? It's not a fancy minecart. It's just a regular old cart that I pull."

"Err, it's faster if I just show you," said Graser. "It'd take too much time to explain."

As the old man watched, Graser took five iron ingots and began crafting something else. It was long and square and seemed to have unseen wheels on the bottom that would allow it to fit right on the rail. It was a minecart. When it was completed, that was exactly where Graser placed it.

"But I don't need any old minecart!" the villager objected. "I need *my* cart. It has sentimental value. Plus, it's the best in my village, so I get lots of esteem from having it."

Graser looked at the impatient old man and crossed his arms. Graser was silent, but his expression said: 'Do you want me to help you or not?' Graser tapped his foot in the sand testily.

"Okay, okay," said the old man. "You do whatever you want to do."

Graser uncrossed his arms and took two more iron ingots out of his pack. He hammered them into a single plate. Then he approached the back of the cart, and handed the metal plate to the old man.

"I'm going to lift the cart again," Graser said.

"But we *can't* lift it," objected the man. "We tried that before."

"I'm only going to lift it an inch," said Graser. "When I do, I want you to slip this iron plate in behind it."

"You're the boss," said the old man. "Actually, what *are* you exactly? You don't look like anyone I've met before."

"Some kind of robot, as far as I know," answered Graser. "I'm actually on a quest to find out who I am and where I came from."

"Ooh, sounds exciting," said the old man.

"I'm just getting started," said Graser. "I've only been on the quest for the better part of this morning."

"Still. . . *I've* never been on a quest," said the man. "And I've had lots of years to do it."

"Hey, it's never to late to start," said Graser. "Now let's get back to the matter at hand. I'm going to life up the cart. One. . . two. . . *three*!"

Graser pushed with all his might on the back of the cart. It was still stuck in the sand, but he did get it to move up a few inches. When he did, the old man slipped the heavy iron plate into the open space.

"Whew," he said. "This is hard work."

"You only had to put that plate in there," Graser said. "I had to move the cart."

The old man rolled his eyes to say Graser's travails did not count for much.

Graser got down on his knees and began scooping up mounds of sand. Then he took a grey, grainy substance out of his inventory and began stacking it next to the sand.

"Hey, what's that?" said the old man.

"Sand," said Graser. "You should know. Your cart's stuck in it."

"No," said the man. "I mean the other stuff."

"Gunpowder," Graser answered seriously.

"Gunpowder?" the villager replied. "What are you messing with *that* for? It's dangerous."

"I'm building a block of TNT," Graser said. "A particularly large one, so it's going to require a whole lot of gunpowder and sand."

The old villager seemed dumbfounded.

"But. . . But. . ."

"Just be patient," Graser said. "I'm almost done."

Graser took the mounds of sand and dynamite and crafted them into one enormous block of TNT. The old man had never seen a block so large. Neither had Graser.

"Okay," Graser said. "I'm going to pull back on the cart even farther this time. I'll need you to stick this TNT beside the metal plate."

"It's not going to explode me, is it?" asked the old man nervously.

Graser thrust the TNT into his ancient hands.

"Not unless I set it off," Graser said with a grin.

Summoning all of his strength, Graser pushed as hard as he could on the back of the cart. It was still irrevocably stuck in the sand, but Graser made just enough headway for the old man to place the TNT. Then Graser relaxed and the cart fell back into place. Graser walked several paces away from the cart, and extended one of his thumbs. He sighted down it like a painter.

"What're you doing now?" the old man said.

"Checking my math," said Graser. "And you know what? I think it all checks out! We're ready to go."

"You *think* it checks out," said the old man. "What happens if it doesn't?"

"I dunno," said Graser. "But probably, your prized cart gets blown up."

"Well that doesn't sound very good," said the man. "What happens if it works out correctly?"

"Here," said Graser. "I'll show you."

Graser walked to the TNT block and ignited it. The fuse began to burn. Graser retreated behind the nearest sand dune. The old man followed. Graser stuck his glowing red eyes over the top of the dune *juuuuust* enough to watch the resulting explosion. It was really, *really* big.

KA-BOOM!

The TNT blast was enormous. It blew sand everywhere. For a moment, both Graser and the old man were unable to see. When the sand cleared, the cart was gone.

"Oh no," said the old man. "You've destroyed it!"

Graser said nothing, but confidently extended a single finger. Then he turned it upwards. The old man's eyes looked to the spot where Graser was pointing. High in the sky above them was a single tan block. As they watched, it slowly got larger. Before long, it was clear what it was. The cart. It had been blown heavenward by the TNT.

"Here's where we see if my math paid off," Graser said.

"Yikes," said the old man, covering his eyes. "I can't bear to watch."

The cart tumbled back toward the Overworld at incredible speed. Graser looked on as it descended at the perfect angle to land on the minecart that was already sitting on the rail tracks. The old man's cart connected with a thud. It was just the right size to sit within the minecart. The momentum rolled the minecart and its new cargo safely along the tracks, across the sand, and back to the safety of the main desert trail.

"Holy cats!" said the old man. "That was amazing. I'll have to look into this 'math' you were talking about. Especially if it lets you do stuff like that."

"Yeah, it's pretty cool," Graser agreed.

They walked over to where the cart had ended up. The old man began to inspect it.

"Not a scratch!" he said.

"The iron plate protected it," Graser said. "Iron will do that."

"You must let me repay you for this kindness," said the man.

"I don't need a reward," Graser said. "I like helping people. Especially when I can do it with crafting."

"Nonsense," the man said. "I have to give you something. Tell me, are you headed east by any chance?"

"I am," said Graser.

"Are you going as far as the Blue Ice Plains Spikes biome?" he pressed.

"There and past it," Graser said.

"Then we shall go together," the man said. "And I will give you your reward when we arrive."

Graser shrugged.

"It looks like I'm powerless to stop you," he said.

"One more thing," the old man said. "I get bored easily. Can you tell me some stories while we walk? My cart doesn't have a radio or anything."

"Um…" Graser began.

"And also, can you pull the cart? My back has been acting up."

"Um..."

"And also, I'm going to just sit in the cart."

Graser sighed again. (Sighing for a robot was never really necessary, but Graser still liked to do it. It seemed the perfect way to express what he was feeling at times like these.)

Seeing there was little else that he could do to change the situation, Graser removed the cart from the railcar and set it back on the trail. The old man climbed inside, and Graser began to pull it down the path. As he pulled, he told the old man stories.

Graser walked for many hours. Soon, the desert gave way to another taiga. Then that gave way to a cold taiga where there were tiny snowflakes fluttering in the air. Graser knew they were getting close to the old man's destination.

The old man, who had been silent for most of the trip, abruptly piped up.

"There!" he said.

Graser looked over his shoulder and saw that the old man was pointing.

Ahead of them loomed the Blue Ice Plains Spikes biome. Like most ice plains spikes biomes, it was composed of snow blocks and giant thin spikes made of ice. Yet unlike its cousins, the spikes on this biome were a deep prismatic blue.

"It's the lapis lazuli deposits in the area," said the old man. "Little trace amounts get caught up in the ice spikes. Over time it builds. Then you're left with what you see here."

"It's beautiful," Graser said. Graser was not, typically, one to dwell on the aesthetics of natural structures in the Overworld. He was too busy thinking about how those structures could be bashed apart and crafted into something cool. But something about the blue ice spikes really took his breath away. He suddenly remembered why he had never travelled farther east than this. It was because having seen these spikes, he frankly doubted that he could find anything more breathtaking.

"That's why I come out here," said the old man, hopping down from the cart.

"To see the spikes?" asked Graser.

"Not to see them—to *sell* them," the old man clarified. "Do you know how much people will pay back in my village for a blue ice spike? Let me save you some time. It's a whole lot."

"Huh," said Graser. "I never thought of that. How do you get the spikes across the desert before they melt?"

"You pack them in snow," the old man said. "I've got a system that works pretty well. The only drawback is that it takes a whole lot of snow. I can only do one ice spike at a time."

"I see," Graser said with a metal grin. "Well this is where we part ways, I'm afraid. I've got to reach Redstone Castle, and it's through this biome."

"Just a minute," said the old man. "I promised you I'd give you a reward in exchange for getting my cart out of the sand. I'm a man who keeps his word. Follow me."

The old man set off across the plain of packed ice and snow. Graser shrugged and followed. Their feet left deep footprints in the snow. (Graser's rather more, because he was much heavier.) Polar bears and white rabbits sometimes spied on the duo from the distant horizon, but always stayed away. Being jet black, Graser stuck out like a sore thumb when walking across a snowy landscape. It was hard for the local animals *not* to notice him.

Eventually, the old man took him to a part of the biome where the ice spikes were tallest and thickest. The old man took a rusty iron pickaxe out of his inventory and began chipping away at the base of a particularly tall spike. As Graser looked on, the towering spike began to wobble back and forth. Then it began to fall.

"*Timberrrrrrrr*!" cried the old man.

Then the seemed to have second thoughts.

"Wait a minute. Ice spikes aren't made of timber. What am I saying? *IIIIIIIIIIIIIIIIIce*!"

No sooner were these words out of his mouth than the towering spike fell to the snow with a thud. The tip of the ice spike was the bluest ice Graser had ever seen. The old man used his pickaxe to carve it into a sharp point. Then he turned and handed the point to Graser.

"This is the most special of all the blue ice spikes," the old man said. "It's very hard. It also seems never to melt, even in the hottest rays of the sun. I wonder if it might be magically, permanently cold. I've never harvested it because I was waiting for a special occasion. I think today is that occasion."

"Thanks," Graser said, turning the icy blue point over in his fingers. "What do I. . . err. . . *do* with it exactly?"

"I dunno," said the old man. "I'm sure you'll figure it out. Now if you'll excuse me, I have to harvest another ice spike, pack it in snow, and haul it back to my village. There's a backlog of customers waiting."

Graser shrugged and placed the blue ice spike into his inventory. Then he retraced his own footsteps in the ice until he found the main trail again. He could hear the old man chipping away at another ice spike in the distance.

As he made his way through the rest of the Blue Ice Spikes biome, the chipping gradually faded away.

Graser soon reached the edge of the biome. Now he had travelled farther from his home than he ever had before. He did not know exactly what he would find when the last of the ice spikes faded away. The mysterious note had said something about Extreme Hills of Sledding. Graser had never been one for sleds. It was an activity he could take or leave. To Graser, it had always seemed there were far funner things you could do with snow than slide around on top of it. For example, you could pack it into snowballs and then hit your friends in the face with those snowballs. Or you could dig a pit and then cover it over with thin layer of snow and laugh when your friend stepped on it and fell inside. In short, for Graser there seemed to be substantially reduced potential for snow-related mischief when you were on a sled.

Soon the spikes in the landscape around him became less frequent, and smaller—not really spikes, but more like tiny nubs of ice. Graser worried more about tripping over them than running into them. Then they faded away entirely and the hills began. Graser had been in Extreme Hills biomes before, but something told him that what he was about to experience was going to be different.

As Graser entered the biome he saw that the hills stretched high enough to touch the clouds above. There were oak and spruce trees growing along the sides of the hills, but they became small and wizened near the tops of the hills simply because there was not enough oxygen and rain to sustain them. The tops of the hills were covered with glistening white snow caps. Graser heard a strange, swift sucking sound. He turned and saw small grey silverfish scuttling about in a valley between the hills. The path beneath Graser's feet led away into the towering hills. He followed it carefully, and was soon swallowed up by the landscape. The hills surrounded him on all sides.

Just as Graser was about to comment that he had not seen any sledding—which you'd expect if you were visiting a place with "Sledding" in its name—Graser noticed a villager at the very tippy-top of the nearest hill. Graser knew that falling from such a height could result in several hearts of damage, so he was concerned when the villager began to suddenly plummet down the side of the hill at a tremendous speed. Instinctively, Graser broke into a run. Yet his robotic heart sank; he knew he would never reach the base of the hill in time to catch the man.

Then the astounding thing happened.

Graser realized the villager was leaving a trail of snow and dirt behind him. This was because he was not actually falling, but riding down the side of the hill on something. Which, Graser quickly concluded, had to be a sled.

Though they were coming from opposite directions, Graser reached the base of the hill just moments after the villager. The villager slowed to a stop amid a great cloud of dust. When the dust cleared, it became apparent that the villager was standing on a kind of long flat sled or surfboard. But that was not entirely right, Graser thought to himself, because there were four square holes near the back of the board.

Suddenly, it struck Graser.

"You're standing on a door!" Graser said to the villager.

The villager stepped off the door. Then he used his foot to flip the door into the air, and caught it with one hand.

"What's it to you, robot?" the villager said rather rudely.

"That's just. . . a strange way to go sledding, I guess," Graser said.

"No it's not," the villager insisted. "It's the normal way."

"Whatever you say," Graser replied, shaking his head.

"Do you need anything else now, or can I go back to sledding?" the villager said derisively, continuing to be rude.

"No," Graser said. "I only ran over because I thought you were falling."

The villager rolled his eyes.

"You're pretty dumb for a robot," the villager said, and began trudging back up the hill.

Graser returned to the path and continued on his way.

"Maybe they should call this the biome of extreme rudeness," Graser said to himself.

He journeyed on deeper into the hills, and soon saw more villagers sledding down the towering hills around him (or else climbing back up after a good sled down). Some of them were also using iron or wooden doors to sled, but others still had found different materials that seemed to work just as well. Long bands of metal. Improvised minecarts. Sign posts. Pressure plates. Even long sheets of stained glass. (Graser couldn't believe they didn't break!) All to propel themselves down the hillsides at terrifying speeds.

As Graser walked through the valleys marveling at the sledders, many of them stopped to look at him. A few even pointed. This may have been because Graser was a strange looking robot, but may also have simply been because he was the only one without a sled.

Just as he was wondering if he should craft a plate and hold it under his arm—just to fit in—Graser rounded a bend in the hills and a village came into view. It had several square houses with flat roofs, a few more with peaked roofs, and copious gardens where crops were growing. This was a bit strange, since villages did not usually spawn in Extreme Hills biomes, so Graser decided to investigate. When he drew closer, he discovered something stranger still.

The village was falling apart. There was no other way to put it. The houses were missing doors and windows. The buildings had holes in many of the walls. Some of the structures were leaning as though they might collapse because so many essential parts had been removed. For a moment, Graser wondered if this might be a zombie village—which were known to be without doors on the houses. But no. Graser could see normal-looking villagers wandering to and fro.

"This is very odd," Graser said to himself.

Graser approached the nearest villager. It was a farmer villager in a brown coat. It looked as though both he and his coat had seen better days.

"What's going on here?" Graser asked the farmer. "Why is your village in such bad shape? Has there been a zombie siege or something?"

"I wish!" said the farmer to Graser's astonishment. "A zombie siege would be a blessing compared to what we have to deal with."

"Huh?" said Graser.

"It's the sledders," the farmer clarified. "They're worse than zombies. They need new sleds so they come to our village to scavenge for parts. They take the doors off our houses, and take the windows out of our window frames. Sometimes they even rip blocks right out of our walls!"

"That's horrible," said Graser.

"You're telling me," said the farmer. "With zombies, they only want to get to you personally. You're safe inside four walls. But these sledders want the walls too!"

"I see," said Graser.

"It's hard enough making living out here," the farmer continued. "For the moment my crops are still untouched, but the moment these people decide they can make a sled out of carrots and beets, it's all over!"

"It looks like everybody's house has been hit pretty bad," Graser said. "Does the whole village have this problem?"

The farmer nodded to say that it was so.

"Is anybody in charge?" asked Graser. "Do you have a policeman—or policewoman—who could try to stop the sledders?"

The farmer thought for a moment.

"We do have a mayor. . ." the farmer said slowly. "But she's very depressed."

"Depressed?" said Graser.

"Yeah," said the farmer. "Wouldn't *you* be?"

He swung his arm wide to indicate the decimation before them.

"Hmm, I think I see your point," said Graser. "Can I try talking to the mayor? Maybe I could help. My name's Graser. I'm from very far away, on the other side of the Blue Ice Plains Spikes. I'm known for helping people."

"I guess you could try," said the farmer cautiously. "Why not? It might at least cheer the mayor up to meet a weird looking robot with glowing eyes."

Graser decided that that might have to do.

The farmer conducted Graser down the central street of the village. At the end of the street was the largest building—a four walled structure with a sign that said CITY HALL over the door. Or rather, it once had said CITY HALL. Now it said C TY HA.

"The sledders took the 'I' and both the 'Ls' too," explained the farmer. "They looked too much like letters you could make a sled out of, I suppose. In retrospect, we should have seen that coming."

The farmer approached the structure and knocked on the stone wall beside the door. He did not knock on the door itself, because it was no longer there. There was nothing but a pair of rusty hinges hanging down from the side of the wall.

"Mayor, there's a visitor to see you!" the farmer called.

"Oh," a voice came back from the gloom within. "Is it someone from a different village, asking me to come and be their mayor instead? That would certainly be nice."

"Come now, mayor," said the farmer, looking at Graser with slight embarrassment. "It's not all that bad."

They went inside. Graser took a torch out of his inventory and handed it to the farmer. Then he took out one for himself. The flickering light of their portable flames showed a municipal office in deep disrepair. There was a broken desk piled high with papers, broken chairs, and broken windows. The tables were also collapsed or upside down. It looked as though the place had not been used for any government work in a very long time.

Seated in the middle of the mess was a woman dressed in black who looked very unhappy indeed. She was seated on a cushion staring at the wall. She did not even look up at her visitors.

"Madame Mayor, this is our guest," said the farmer. "He comes from far away and his name is Graser. He says he thinks he could help. You know, with the sledders."

"I'll believe that when I see it," said the mayor, who continued to see only the wall before her.

"Can you tell me how this happened?" Graser asked. "Was it always like this?"

For a moment, no answer came. The Graser heard a very strange sound, almost like a mouse in distress. Suddenly, he realized that the tiny squeaks were the mayor crying.

After a moment, the mayor collected herself, dried her eyes, and turned around to face her visitors. She looked like a pleasant woman, but who circumstances had taken to the end of her rope.

"I'm sorry," she said. "It's just that I feel awful when I think about what this place has become. It used to be a perfectly nice and normal village. I loved being mayor of it. Then one day, out of the blue, some people showed up and asked if there were rules about sledding down the extreme hills. I say no. . . goodness help me! . . .because they're weren't. It had never occurred to any of us to sled. We don't tend to be a thrill seeking bunch. We told the people it would be okay for them to sled if they wanted to. Nobody thought anything would come of it. If anything, people said it might be good for our little village. That it would bring in tourism, and so forth. Anyhow, the sledders must have started to tell their friends about the hills, because their number increased exponentially. At first there were just a few of them— which was fine—but then there got to be hundreds! Lots and lots! Now, on days when the weather is nice, they can run into the thousands! It wouldn't be so bad if they all showed up with their own sleds, but they don't. So they just grab whatever's around. It's just ruined our village. People say 'Why craft anything? The sledders will just tear it apart.' And they're right!"

The mayor's chin fell to her chest. She looked utterly despondent.

"Did you try asking the sledders *not* to take stuff to make sleds out of it?" Graser asked delicately.

"Oh believe me, I did," said the mayor. "That was my campaign slogan in the last election. 'Vote for me and I will ask very nicely for the sledders not to take our things,' it went. I won by a landslide. But then it didn't work. The sledders did not listen to me. They kept right on scavenging our homes for parts. Now nobody wants to live in the village anymore. We're really unpopular. Except with the sledders."

Graser tried to think of how he could help the village. Graser wasn't known for always having the brightest ideas, but sometimes when he thought about something for long enough he could figure it out. Other times, Graser found the solution to problems came through sheer trial and error. Mostly error.

"Let me ask you another question," Graser said to the mayor. "Is you goal to get rid of the sledders entirely? Because we could probably figure out a way to do that. We could release a bunch of zombies for example."

"No no no," said the mayor, shaking her head. "The zombies would chase us off too. And anyway, it's not really the sledders we mind *per se*, it's their habit of scavenging. I don't even think an outbreak of zombies would be enough to get rid of them. Now, this biome is known for the sledders. If people came here and didn't see them, they'd be disappointed."

"In that case, I have an idea," Graser said.

"You do?" said the mayor, sounding as though she'd heard that line before. (Graser thought she probably had.)

"Yes," Graser continued. "The thing about the doors and bits of cottage—and all the other things—that the sledders are using right now. . . is that they don't make very good sleds, do they? I'm no expert, but even I can see that the four holes in a typical door are going to make for a pretty bumpy ride down the side of a hill."

"I guess that's true," said the mayor. "So what are you suggesting?"

"We need to craft sleds for the sledders," Graser said. "We need to craft very, *very* good ones. If they have good, durable sleds, the sledders won't want to salvage your town for parts."

"But where are we going to get the personnel for that?" cried the mayor. "Not to mention the cost!?!?"

"I didn't say we would give them away," said Graser. "You can sell the sleds. Then you can use the money to repair your town."

"Oh," said the mayor. "I never thought of that."

"And I'll get you started by crafting the first sled," Graser pledged.

"Err, how exactly do you do that?" inquired the farmer, who was listening intently.

"I dunno," said Graser. "I never did it before."

Graser walked outside of the CT Y HA, put his hands on his robotic hips, and surveyed the landscape around him. He had no idea what a good sled would be made of. In a way, this was liberating. *All* choices were open to him.

Graser knew that, unlike him, most people were made of flesh and blood. And flesh was something that could be easily bruised if you went down a hill to fast on a sled. Probably, it would be good to make sure flesh was cushioned with something soft.

On the other side of the coin, soft things wouldn't withstand a lot of trips down a hillside. The sleds would also need to be strong and durable. Smooth too, Graser thought. They needed to be able to slide over snow and grass alike.

"Where should we start?" asked a voice.

Graser looked and saw that the doughty farmer had joined him.

"Let's take stock of what we have to work with in the area," Graser said, looking across the biome. "I see that we've got oak trees and spruce trees around here. And some pretty flowers growing down by the water. Is there anything else around here I don't know about?"

"Ooh, yes," said the farmer. "The ground is full of emerald ore. I only know that because I sometimes hit it when I'm churning the soil on my farm. It's really annoying. I'm not much good with a pickaxe, and it takes me forever to break it up."

A plan began to solidify in Graser's mind.

"Can you take me to one of these ore deposits?" he asked the farmer.

"You want to go to a small one or a big one?" the farmer asked.

"The biggest you got," replied Graser.

The farmer marched them to a spot a few yards past the village proper, in the shadow of an imposing hill. Above them, sledders frolicked, oblivious to their presence.

"It may not look like much," the farmer said. "But I tried digging there once. *Once.* It's solid ore all the way down."

"Perfect," Graser said, and took a diamond pickaxe out of his inventory.

Graser began chipping away at the upper crust of the land. Sure enough, after just a couple of whacks, it gave way to reveal emerald ore. Graser mined it until he had a sizeable amount in his inventory. Something told him he'd only just scratched the surface of how much was in this deposit. Then Graser took the ore, combined it with coal, and smelted it into a number of glistening emeralds.

"Ooh," said the farmer. "Pretty!"

Next Graser walked to the nearest birch tree and began chopping away at it. He hacked and hacked. It was a very tall tree, and soon Graser was surrounded by chunks of wood. He quickly crafted these into wood planks.

"Wow," said the farmer, admiring his work. "You could be a carpenter."

Graser put the planks into his inventory and headed off to a pool of water in the middle of the nearest valley. Around it, several forms of flower grew. Graser began to pick them.

"This is where I pick flowers for my wife," the farmer said. "Blue Orchids are her favorite. Make sure you leave a few of those in the ground for her, okay?"

"No problem," said Graser with a robotic grin. "I'll be sure to do that."

When he had picked a huge armful of the flowers, Graser set all his ingredients before him: the flowers, the wooden planks, and the emeralds. He started by fashioning the planks together into a long shape that was decidedly sled-like.

"Ooh," said the farmer. "I think I see where this is going."

Next Graser took the emeralds and polished them until they were perfectly smooth. After this was done, he affixed them to the bottom of the sled. Before long, the entire underside was a bright emerald green.

"Hmm," said the farmer. "Maybe I *don't* see where this is going. Very strange to have a jeweled sled."

Ignoring the farmer, Graser continued working. He took the flowers and attached them to the upper part of the sled, on the opposite side from the emeralds. It was clear the farmer did not even know what to think at this point. He sat down and began scratching his head. He had never seen anything like this.

"Well. . . it's a sled," the farmer said cautiously. "It's just that it's about the weirdest sled I ever came across."

"Let me take you through it," said Graser, placing his creation on the ground. "The planks make the body of the sled; that's no mystery. But the polished emeralds on the bottom are much smoother than wood. The emeralds will slide over snow and ice, but also down grassy hills too. It'll go much faster than a sled made of birch alone. The emeralds are also very strong, and will keep the sled from breaking if it goes over something hard. These sleds will last for years."

"What about the flowers?" said the farmer.

"Those serve as extra padding," said Graser. "It makes the ride down the hill a whole lot easier on your backside."

"That ought to be nice," said the farmer.

"Here," said Graser, picking up the sled once more, "let's go find some sledders to show it to."

Graser slowly turned around in a slow circle, holding a hand above his glowing eyes to survey the horizon. He found the extreme hill with the largest group of sledders going up and down it. Graser moseyed over, proudly carrying his new creation. As Graser began to climb the side of the hill, the sunlight hit the emeralds on the underside of the sled and made them sparkle wildly. Heads turned. Many of the sledders began to whisper. Who was this strange black robot, and who was he trying to impress with an emerald-studded sled?

Graser reached a small crowd of perhaps 20 or 30 sledders at the top of the hill, waiting their turn to take the ride down. They looked him over. Graser held up a hand and cleared his throat. Graser had never tried to sell anything before, but he had seen plenty of vendors in villages and other places. It didn't seem like there was much of a trick to it.

"Hey everybody!" Graser said to the sledders. "Check this out! I've got an amazing new sled that's going to change sledding forever. It gives you a cushioned ride, has a strong underside made of emeralds, and—here's the best part—you can buy it from me instead of having to make a sled yourself by tearing a villager's home apart. What do you say?"

Graser let his mouth hang open expectantly. The sledders did not move closer to look at the sled. In fact, they didn't move forward at all. Instead, they looked at Graser like he had two heads.

"Emeralds on the *bottom* of the sled," someone whispered dismissively. "People can't even see them there. It entirely defeats the purpose!"

"Paying for a sled?" said someone else in the crowd. "Why would I pay for one when I can make my own. . .preferably out of some stupid villager's house."

Graser began to sense that his audience did not immediately see the features and benefits of his creation.

"I see you're not convinced," Graser told them. "In that case, I think a demonstration is in order."

Graser took the sled and walked to the edge of the hilltop. The crowd parted for him. Graser set the sled firmly into the snow and climbed aboard. The farmer nervously followed but stopped short of the sled.

"Psst," said the farmer. "Have you ever ridden a sled before?"

Graser thought for a moment.

"Actually, no," Graser said. "I don't think I have."

"Well be careful," the farmer whispered. "If you're not, you can run into a tree or worse. Sleds go awfully fast. And those are the ones that *don't* have polished emeralds on the undersides."

"How hard can it be?" said Graser. "I'm sure I'll be fine."

Graser looked around. The sledders were watching expectantly. It was now or never.

"Okay," shouted Graser. "You're all about to see what a phenomenal sled this really is. One. . . two. . . three!"

Graser pushed off. Suddenly, the world around him seemed to have transformed into a blur. He blinked his eyes rapidly, wondering if he was seeing things. However, he quickly realized that this blur was actually a side effect of travelling very, very fast. There was also a sound. A tremendous "woosh" that Graser realized was the noise made by the front of his sled cutting into the snow and kicking it up. After just a couple of moments, the "woosh" changed to a low rumble. This happened because Graser's sled had already left the snowy peak of the hill and was now cruising across and grass and mud that comprised the lower hillside. Suddenly, Graser noticed a bright flash of blue in front of him that seemed to grow exponentially larger by the moment. He seemed to be heading directly for it.

Before Graser could think about correcting his course, the sled slammed into the wide pool of blue. It was water, and the sled skimmered across the top for a few moments before sinking down into it. Graser had descended the hillside in a flash, and crashed right into a pool at the bottom of the valley. (Which, considering all the other things there were to crash into, left Graser feeling very lucky indeed.) Graser held his breath and dog-paddled back to shore with one hand, while gripping the sled in the other.

He reached the land again and spent a moment recovering. Because he was a robot, Graser did not get "out of breath" in the same way humans did, but what he had just experienced was still very bewildering. He wanted to take a moment to process it.

As Graser caught his virtual breath, the sledders stampeded down the hill in his direction. For a moment, this alarmed Graser. He thought they might be upset with him for some reason. Then he saw the expressions on their faces and realized he had nothing to fear.

"I'll give you a hundred blocks of diamond for that sled!" shouted the sledder at the head of the pack.

"No," said another. "Don't sell to him. Sell to me! I'll give you a hundred and fifty diamond blocks for it."

Then someone farther back shouted: "I'll make it two hundred!"

Graser smiled. When the mob of sledders finally reached him, he had to hold his sled high to keep them from grabbing it out of his hands.
"This sled has a very special price," Graser said.

"What?" pled one of the crowd. "Just tell me and I'll pay it."

"This sled will be given to whomever can repair the city hall in the village to how it was before you plundered it for sledding parts," Graser said.

"I can do that," exclaimed a member of the group, and sprinted away. Several others followed him, perhaps hoping to be rewarded with a part of the sled, or at least a few turns on it, if they helped out with the rebuilding.

The remaining sledders looked disappointed. Some even kicked at the dirt in anger.

"Now, now," said Graser. "Don't get upset. This sled is just a prototype. We'll be making lots and lots of them."

Smiles spread across the faces of the assembled crowd.

"You will!?!" they asked expectantly.

"Well. . . *he* will," Graser said. He pointed to the back of the crowd to where the farmer was rushing to catch up. The sledders looked at the farmer doubtfully.

"Er, can I talk to you for a second?" the farmer said to Graser.

Graser nodded, and they took a slow saunter together around the lake at the bottom of the valley. The crowd of sledders stayed where they were—still confused, excited, and determined to get one of those emerald-bottomed sleds for themselves.

"What are you talking about?" the farmer whispered. "I don't know how to make those sleds."

"You just watched me do it," Graser reminded him. "You know what all the ingredients are, and in what quantities."

"Yes, but I'm not a crafter," the farmer objected.

"You are bound to have some crafters in your village," Graser said.

"Now that you mention it, I suppose we do have a few crafters around," the farmer conceded.

"Here's what you do," Graser instructed him. "Tell your crafters how I built my sled, and have them follow my steps exactly. All of the resources you need are found in plentiful amounts in this biome, so it won't cost you anything. After you make the sleds, don't give them away. Sell them to the sledders in exchange for rebuilding your town. After the town is fixed up, you can take other things in exchange for the sleds. Then you can use that wealth to maintain your hills, and maybe hire someone to make sure that no other sledders take parts that don't belong to them."

"Hey," said the farmer. "That's not a bad idea."

"Sometimes I have good ones," Graser said modestly. "If these emerald sleds catch on like I think they will, you won't *need* to convince people not to make their own. They'll want to hold out for one of yours."

"I like it!" said the farmer. "Why don't we go and tell the mayor about this new plan. It's sure to cheer her up."

"Okay," said Grazer. "But then I really must be on my way. I'm so excited to reach Redstone Castle, and I think I'm very close."

They walked the rest of the way around the lake to where the expectant crowd of sledders was still waiting. The sledders were talking excitedly about how fast Graser's sled had gone, and conjecturing about what tricks it might be able to do when ridden by an expert. As Graser and the farmer drew close, they began to clamor for more.

"I have good news," Graser said, raising his metal hands to silence them. "More sleds will be available for sale tomorrow morning bright and early in the village. I'd advise anybody wanting to purchase one to bring his or her crafting tools, or else a whole lot of valuable blocks."

The excited sledders raced off so quickly that half of them seemed to run into one another, knocking each other over in their excitement to fetch the means with which to buy a sled of their own. After the crowd dispersed, Graser and the farmer walked back to the village. They walked down the main street until they reached the C TY HA. There, they beheld a very strange sight. The mayor was standing on the steps holding a broom. She used it to shoo away the ten or so sledders who took turns trying to approach.

"We just want to help," pled one of the sledders.

"Yes," said another. "We want to help you repair this building."

"Get outta here!" cried the mayor, waving her broom angrily. "I know your tricks. You've stolen pieces of this building before. I'm not about to let you do it again!"

Graser tried to stifle a laugh. The farmer ran forward and convinced the mayor to lower her broom.

"It's okay, mayor," the farmer said. "These people are here to help!"

"But they're *sledders*," said the mayor. She pronounced this final word as if it was most distasteful.

"It's because they're sledders that they want to help!" said the farmer. He went on to summarize the way that Graser had built the emerald sled, and the bargain that he had struck with the sledders. The mayor's eyes went wide as she listened. It was clearly difficult for her to believe what she was hearing.

"So all we have to do is build more of these sleds like Graser did, and the sledders will repair the damage they've done?" she asked when the farmer had finished.

"And after that they'll give us money," the farmer said.

"I have a feeling it will be lots and lots of money," added Graser. "Your village is about to go from the laughingstock of the Overworld to an object of envy for villages everywhere. Do you think you'll be able to handle this reversal of fortune?"

"Eh," said the mayor. "We'll manage."

Graser laughed.

"If we're through now, I need to be on my way," Graser added. "I'm on an important quest."

"Just a second," said the mayor. "Come inside with me. You have given our village a great gift. It's only appropriate for me to give you something in return."

Graser was impatient to be on his way, but he thought it would be rude to turn down the mayor. He followed her into the dilapidated city hall. With the mayor (and her broom) no longer occupying the front steps, the sledders moved in and began to repair the structure.

The mayor rifled through the dusty, broken furniture in her office until she came upon an ancient chest. She opened it and reached inside.

"Maybe you've heard of receiving the key to the city?" the mayor said to Graser. "I'm afraid the best I can do is give you the key to the village."

The mayor held aloft a shiny gold key. Though everything in her office seemed dusty and dim, the key sparkled as though newly polished. Graser wondered if some form of magic might not be involved.

"This key predates the village," the mayor explained. "My mother, who was the first mayor, brought it with her when she founded our village. She said it had been given to her by her mother in turn."

"Is it magic?" Graser asked, accepting the incandescent key from the mayor. "Because it kind of looks magic."

It was the mayor's turn to laugh.

"Funny you should say that," the mayor replied. "I've been asked that many times. While the key has no specific magical power that I know of, it has a way of coming in handy whenever it is needed. I can say no more than that. When the problem with the sledders first started, I thought somehow the key would come in handy for stopping them. Now, I think it was meant for passing on to you."

"Thanks," said Graser, carefully placing the shiny key into his inventory. "I promise to take good care of it."

Once outside again, Graser could see that the sledders were already working wonders. The CITY HALL now said CITY HA now, which was not completely correct, but still an improvement. The mayor and the farmer walked Graser to the edge of town.

"Where are you off to now?" the farmer asked. "You said something about a castle?"

"I'm trying to find out who created me," Graser answered. "Apparently, the answer lies in a place called Redstone Castle, directly east of here."

"Hmm, that's weird," said the farmer.

"What is?" asked Graser.

"That I've never heard of it," said the farmer. "You'd think I'd know if there were a castle around here. Mayor, do you know anything about a castle?"

The mayor shook her head. For a moment, this worried Graser. Had he been sent all this way across the Overworld in vain?

Then the mayor said: "But you mentioned that its name is 'Redstone Castle' correct?"

Graser nodded.

"Odd," said the mayor. "I *have* seen zombies and skeletons moving an awful lot of redstone recently. And they're always headed east with it. Do you think zombies and skeletons could have created you?"

"Err, I dunno," said Graser. "I sure hope not. They're jerks. They're always terrorizing the villages near me, and they used to always try to get into my palace. The idea that they were involved in creating me is not a pleasant one."

"Oh," said the mayor. "Well then forget I said anything. There are other possibilities too. Maybe whoever created you just employs the zombies and skeletons. Or maybe. . . Or maybe. . ."

The mayor trailed off. his left Graser feeling a bit uneasy. Zombies and skeletons carrying redstone? What in the Overworld did that portend? As he waved goodbye to the farmer and the mayor—and set off east once more—Graser found that he now had more questions than answers.

Graser passed out of the Hills of Extreme Sledding and into a flat plains biome. It was filled with tall grass, flowers, and just a couple of tiny trees. Packs of wild horses and donkeys cavorted in the distance. The sun shone down brightly in a nearly cloudless sky.

Just as Graser was wondering how much further it might be, he caught a glint of red on the horizon. It was a very specific shade of red. The summer sun shining down upon it left little room for doubt. As Graser drew closer, the red grew before him. It was now unmistakable. Redstone. More of it than Graser had ever seen in one place. (And Graser had seen a lot of things.) So much redstone that blocks of it were thrust high into the sky.

It was indeed a castle, Graser soon realized to his relief. It was composed of two large towers, and a large cubed central keep. (It was not very creative as castle designs went, but Grazer let that slide.) The flat top of the castle wall was covered with crenulated parapets. In the center of the castle was an enormous door. It was shut, and there seemed to be no discernable handle or keyhole. As Graser neared, it seemed to him that a very lifelike animal had been carved beside the front of the door—a cat of some sort.

"Well, the note wasn't lying," Graser said to himself. "At least the place exists. Now all I need to do is figure a way to get inside. I wonder what these 'mysteries' that the note talked about are going to be. But first things first. I need to find a way in."

Suddenly, a high-pitched voice said: "When you find it, would you let me know too?"

Graser looked all around, unable to see who or what was addressing him. Had the castle itself talked?

"Hey," said the voice. "Down here."

Graser looked down. It was the cat statue.

"Whoa," said Graser. "A talking statue."

"I'm not a statue," it said. "I'm an ocelot. I just look like I'm made of redstone because I've got so much redstone dust all over me."

"Whoa," said Graser. "A talking ocelot."

"Err, I guess you've got me there," the ocelot said. It shook itself back and forth. Redstone dust fell to the ground all around it.

"How is it you can talk?" Graser asked.

"Lots of ocelots can talk," it replied. "Most of the time, we just don't *feel* like it."

"Oh," said Graser. "Why are you talking to me now?"

"Because I'll take all the help I can get," the ocelot said. "There used to be a pool here, right where this castle has been erected. It was where I kept all of my best fish. Pools are like iceboxes for ocelots. Sometimes you catch more fish than you can eat, so you keep them in a nice big pool. I was really looking forward to eating all the fish I'd stored here! The other day when I came back from a fishing trip, I saw a whole bunch of construction going on. I couldn't figure out why anybody was building anything here. I hoped the builders would finish whatever they were building and go away soon. I decided to go out and hunt some more, and then come back later. That was a big mistake! When I returned, they had built this redstone monstrosity *over* my favorite pool. Now I can't get to all my yummy fish I've saved! It's very upsetting."

"Gee," Graser said. "That's lousy. Are you sure the fish are still down there? Maybe they filled in the pool when they built the castle."

"No!" insisted the ocelot. "I know they're there. I can smell them. When the wind dies down and it's very quiet, I can even hear them splashing. This castle got built *over* the pool. I think if I could somehow get inside, I might be able to find a way down and recover them."

"Interesting," said Graser. "I came here because a note told me that there were mysteries in this castle, and that if I solved them, I'd learn who built me."

"That's odd," said the ocelot. "A lot odder than a talking ocelot, if you ask me."

"If I can find a way inside the castle, you can certainly come with me," said Graser. "Maybe finding the entrance is the first mystery!"

"Let me save you some time," said the Ocelot. "There's no way in. The door doesn't open. I've trying prying it, scratching it with my claws, and even shouting at it. Nothing gets it to open up. I've also tried digging underneath the castle. No dice there, either. Whoever crafted it sunk blocks down into the ground to make a solid foundation. I'm not strong enough to get through."

Graser put his hand on his chin and carefully considered his options. As an expert crafter with the best possible tools in his inventory, Graser knew it would be no trouble at all to produce his diamond pickaxe and begin smashing through the redstone walls. However, something in the wording of the note told him that this might not be the best thing to do. He was supposed to be here to solve mysteries, not bash a castle apart. If whoever (or whatever) had written the note felt like Graser had "cheated" they might not tell him who his creator was.

"Hmm," said Graser. "There's got to be a way inside. I'm sure of it."

Graser walked around the edges of the castle, making a long, slow circuit. The ocelot tagged along at his heels. Graser looked closely at each redstone brick, looking for an imperfection that could signal a trap door or a weakness to exploit. His glowing red eyes saw nothing out of the ordinary. Soon, they had arrived once more at the front.

"See," said the ocelot smugly. "No way in."

Graser studied the door for a moment. Suddenly, something occurred to him.

"There's no chance you've tried *knocking* on the door, is there?" asked Graser.

"*Knocking* on it?" said the ocelot, in apparent disgust. "You mean like a person—or a. . . a. . . *non-ocelot*—might do?"

"It *is* customary," Graser pointed out.

Graser walked up to the front of the castle and knocked loudly on the door three times.

"Whatever," the ocelot said dismissively. "You're just wasting your time."

No sooner were these words out of the creature's mouth than there was a great and sudden grinding sound, as if something very heavy were being pushed across a flat stone floor. To the ocelot's amazement, the great redstone door of the castle began to move. It opened to reveal a stone brick corridor leading away into sheer blackness beyond. When the door had opened completely, the grinding sound stopped.

"Neat!" said Graser. "It must be pressure-plated operated somehow. . .I'm just not sure how! And the door's done with gears. How cool."

The ocelot remained thoughtfully nonplussed.

"So, are we going inside or what?" the ocelot said.

"We?" asked Graser. "Does that mean you're coming with me? I always wanted a friendly kitty cat for a pet."

"I'm nobody's pet!" the ocelot shot back. "Ocelots are proud and independent. I'm just interested in getting back to my pool of delicious fish. That's the only reason I want to go inside with you."

"That's just what a pet would say," Graser pronounced confidently.

"What?" said the ocelot. "No it isn't."

Graser shrugged. (He still thought it was what a pet would say.)

"Anyhow, you should go first down the long, scary tunnel that goes inside the castle," the beast continued. "I'll be walking right behind you."

"But not like a pet, right?" said Graser. "Like a proud independent ocelot."

"Now you've got it," the ocelot said.

Graser shrugged a second time and set off down the dark tunnel that led into Redstone Castle.

The interior of the tunnel was very dark. The walls were jet black.

"What is this, obsidian?" asked the ocelot.

"No, it's stone brick," said Graser. "It just looks like obsidian because it's so dark. Here, maybe this will help."

Graser's eyes suddenly began to glow slightly brighter than normal. It was enough to illuminate the walls of the corridor.

"Ahh," said the ocelot. "That's much better."

"I thought cats could see in the dark," said Graser.

"Hey, telling apart different blocks isn't my forte," replied the ocelot.

"What would you say *is* your forte?" Graser asked.

"You know," said the ocelot. "Jumping around and catching mice and fish and meowing. Awesome stuff like that."

Graser nodded seriously to say he understood.

Abruptly, they began to detect an eerie red glow at the end of the corridor. It was decidedly different from the one cast by Graser's eyes.

"What's that?" whispered the ocelot.

"I dunno," Graser said. "A light of some sort. Looks like two of them. Could be torches. Or glowstones."

"It's scary," said the ocelot.

"Don't worry," said Graser. "I don't think it will seem so scary when we get closer to it."

Graser was wrong. It got much, *much* scarier.

At the end of the hallway was a room with a high ceiling. In the center of the room was an enormous structure made of bone blocks, probably formed with bone meal from fossils. The sculpture formed the shape of an enormous skull. The skull's mouth was open wide, as though it were very hungry. The skull's empty eye sockets had been covered over with red stained glass. Behind them had been placed several lit torches. The overall effect was staring into the head of a great angry giant.

"Oops," said Graser. "Looks like I was wrong. This is *totally* scary."

"Maybe we should leave," suggested the ocelot, looking around nervously. "I don't even like fish all that much. I was thinking of switching to chicken anyway. Much easier to catch."

"Now, now," said Graser. "We've come this far. There must be another mystery for us to solve."

A voice that sounded like two stones grinding together came out of the darkness.

"There is," it said.

The ocelot was so startled that it jumped up into Graser's arms. Graser was less startled by the voice, and more started by the ocelot. He carefully lowered the shaking beast back to the ground.

"Who said that?" Graser asked the darkness. "It wasn't the big skull. I didn't see its mouth move."

"It was me," the chalky voice said.

A form emerged from the shadows to the side of the great skull. It was short and bony and bone-white. A skeleton. It wore a quiver of arrows over its shoulder, and held a bow in one of its hands.

"Who are you?" Graser asked. He did not feel particularly threatened. A single skeleton would be no problem to defeat in combat for a talented, tough crafter like Graser. Also, now that Graser looked the skeleton up and down, he noticed that it did not look completely "grown" or whatever skeletons were. This one seemed more like a teenager.

"I'm Brian," the bony figure answered. "Brian the skeleton. And you must be Graser. They didn't tell me you'd have a cat."

"I'm not a cat, I'm an ocelot," protested the ocelot. "And I don't belong to Graser. I'm totally my own man!"

"Whatever you say," said Brian.

"What am I supposed to do here?" Graser asked Brian. "Why is there a giant skull in this room?"

"It's a test," Brian explained. "More specifically, it's a kind of a riddle that you have to solve. If you solve it, the way before you will open and you can proceed deeper inside the castle. My job is to tell you the riddle. I'm very important."

"Wait," said Graser, waving his metal hand as if to physically dispel the confusion in the air. "How did you get here? Who are you? Were you put here by the person who created me?"

"I'm not allowed to answer any questions like that," said Brian. "They were very particular on that point."

"Who was?" said Graser.

Brian clapped his hand over his mouth and shook his head.

"Sorry," he said. "You won't get any answers from me. Just a riddle."

"Fine," said Graser. "Shoot."

"Okay," said Brian, clearing his throat. "Here's the riddle: 'What do skeletons want?'"

Graser waited for more. Then he slowly looked over at the ocelot. The ocelot was looking at him. Its expression said it had no idea, either.

"*That's* the riddle?" Graser said.

Brian nodded his bony head enthusiastically.

"If you think you know the answer, you're supposed to put it inside of the giant skull's mouth," said Brian.

"That seems needlessly dramatic," Graser pointed out.

"I guess it is a little dramatic, yeah," Brian agreed.

"Wait a minute," said the ocelot. "Skeletons like lots of things. They like attacking villagers and shooting people with arrows and being jerks. How can you put being a jerk inside that skull's mouth?"

Brian shrugged his bony shoulders.

Graser sat down on his haunches and tried to think. What did skeletons want? It was an interesting question. He knew they were territorial, and he knew they were likely to launch an arrow at you if you got too close. But was there some sort of goal beyond that? Some sort of endgame to their activities? Graser was sure he'd never heard about one.

The ocelot curled itself next to Graser.

"What do you think?" the feline asked.

"I don't know," Graser replied honestly. "I've never heard of anything that made a skeleton happy. Whatever you do, they always act about the same. By which I mean, they act like they want to shoot you with an arrow."

"Maybe *he* knows," the ocelot suggested, gesturing with a paw to the young skeleton who waited for them.

"Yeah," said Graser. "Maybe he does."

Graser stood back up and walked over to Brian.

"Ooh," said Brian. "Do you have the answer already? That was fast."

Graser ignored this.

"Can I ask you some questions?" Graser said.

"I can't give you any hints about the riddle, if that's what you mean," said Brian. "To tell you the truth, I don't even know the answer. They didn't tell me."

"But how can you not know what skeletons want?" asked the ocelot. "You're a skeleton."

"Well. . ." the skeleton sputtered. "I mean. . . I know what *I* want, sure. But I can't speak about all skeletons in general. . ."

"I think. . ." Graser interjected before the skeleton could continue, "you're all turned around on the subject of speaking with us. I think you're clearly supposed to talk to us. It's in your job description. In fact, you'd probably get in trouble if you *didn't* talk to us."

"Huh?" said Brian. "What do you mean?"

"It's your job to tell us the riddle, correct?" said Graser.

The skeleton nodded.

"Well then, see? That's talking to us. So talking to us is your job."

"But they said I was only supposed to do that much," Brian said.

"But to answer the riddle, we have to understand the riddle," continued Graser. "When we ask you questions, and you answer them, you're really just helping to tell us the riddle more fully."

"Oh," said the skeleton. "I guess. . . I never thought about it like that. You might be right. Whew! That's a load off my mind. It was so boring standing here waiting for you to arrive. Nothing to do but shoot arrows at the wall. I was hoping I'd get to talk to you when you arrived. Now I guess I can."

Graser gave the ocelot a quick wink.

"Great," said Graser. "So let's talk."

"Ooh, okay," the skeleton said. "What about?"

"You seem like a very interesting person. . . I mean, skeleton," said Graser. "I think we should talk about you."

"Really?" said the skeleton, obviously feeling flattered. Skeletons had no lips, but it seemed to Graser that something like a smile flashed across Brian's bony skull.

"Yes," said Graser. "Isn't that right, ocelot."

"Oh, yes," said the ocelot, playing along. "Frightfully interesting. I always wanted hear all about what it's like to be a skeleton guard."

Now Graser was sure he saw Brian's bony cheeks blushing a little.

"So start by telling us about your big, scary bow," Graser said. (In truth, the skeleton's bow was not either of those things. It was small and puny, and Graser guessed any arrows fired from it would be likely to deflect right off of him.)

"Yes, my bow," Brian said. "I love shooting it. All skeletons do. You can shoot at inanimate objects when there's no other choice. But then you can also shoot at other mobs. But the best—the very best thing of all—is to shoot at crafters."

"Any why do you do that?" Graser pressed. "Why shoot at them?"

"Well. . . it's the biggest challenge, I suppose," Brian said after a moment's consideration. "They often wear armor—like those big diamond boots you've got on—and they sometimes even fight back. Many a skeleton has been lost to the sword of an angry crafter."

"So when you're shooting at the crafter, is your goal to make them reach zero hearts and die?" said Graser.

"It sounds very distasteful when you just blurt it out like that," replied Brian. "But yes, that is the general idea."

"And why do you want crafters to be dead?" Graser asked. "What happens after that?"

Brian but his hand on his chin and drummed his bony fingers for a moment.

"Lessee. . ." Brian said. "I guess after the crafter died it would get buried or just decompose where it was. Certain mobs might come and eat the crafter's leftover fleshy parts. Pretty soon, there'd be nothing left but a. . . but a. . ."

"But what?" asked Graser.

"A skeleton," said Brian. He smacked himself on the skull, as though this profound insight had never before occurred to him.

"So what skeletons want. . . is to create more skeletons," Graser said with great satisfaction.

"What?" said Brian, still bewildered. "No. I mean, could be? Maybe?"

"Sorry about this," said Graser. "But I'm going to need your help for this next part, Brian. Whether you want to lend it or not."

Graser approached the skeleton and grabbed it around the waist. (This was easy to do, because it consisted of only a spine.) Then Graser pinned the surprised skeleton's arms behind its back and began to push it forward.

"March," said Graser.

"Ow!" said Brian. "Hey, that hurts. What's the big idea?"

"I need you to go and stand inside the mouth of that giant skull," said Graser. "If the thing that skeletons want is to make more skeletons—and the riddle asks me to place the thing that skeletons want inside the skull's mouth—then I need to put a skeleton in there. I don't see any other skeletons around right now, do you?"

"Err, no," said Brian, allowing himself to be pushed forward.

Graser placed Brian inside the mouth of the skeleton and stepped away.

"Now stay in there," Graser said. "Let's see if something happens."

"Fine," Brian said defensively. "But did you have to pin my arms like that?"

"I think a lot of other crafters would have smashed you with a diamond sword and then just thrown your individual bones in there," Graser pointed out.

Brian's perspective abruptly changed, and he began to feel that he might have actually gotten off easy. As Brian pondered worse fates, there was suddenly a loud noise. It was very similar to the sound the castle had made when Graser had knocked upon the front door. The glowing eyes of the great skull suddenly changed color from red to green. Graser realized that a colored glass in front of them had shifted mechanically. Then the giant skull's mouth opened even wider, and a wall in back of it shifted. When the dust had settled—for all this kicked up no small amount of it—there was revealed to be a redstone corridor leading away. Graser thought it looked like the giant skull's throat.

"Hey, would you look at that!" said Brian, turning around. "I guess I *was* the answer! I've never been the answer to anything before."

Graser felt a sudden clenching on his mechanical leg. It was the ocelot gripping tightly.

"I'm not sure I want to go down there," said the ocelot nervously. "It looks like the skull will be eating us. It's scary and. . . and. . . "

The ocelot paused and sniffed at the air.

"And what?" asked Graser.

"And. . . I smell fish!" said the ocelot, immediately releasing Graser's leg. "I smell delicious, wonderful fish down that corridor ahead. Let's go. C'mon!!!"

And with that, the ocelot urged Graser forward.

"Fine," said Graser. "I'm going."

"Oh," said Brian as Graser brushed past. "I guess I'll just say here then? Stare at the wall some more?"

There was a tinge of sadness in the young skeleton's voice. It was clear he did not relish the idea of being left alone.

"Do you want to come with us?" Graser asked.

"Could I?" said Brian excitedly, clasping his bony fingers together. "That would be wonderful!"

"You have to promise not to shoot anybody with arrows—unless I tell you to—and no other typical skeleton aggressiveness," Graser cautioned.

"No problem," said Brian. "I promise."

"All right then," said Graser, and the three of them ventured forward into the redstone throat of the skeleton to whatever tests might lay beyond.

It was a long corridor. All redstone. Sconces bearing torches had been thoughtfully set along the walls every few feet, but other than that there was little to see.

The skeleton and the ocelot kept back, a couple of paces behind Graser.

"You know," Brian said. "There are certain skeletons who like to ride things. Spiders, for instance. They're called spider jockeys. Apparently, it's a whole lot of fun for both the skeleton and the spider."

The ocelot turned up its nose.

"If you're asking if you can ride me, the answer is no," the ocelot said sternly.

"But my feet are hurting from all this walking," Brian said. "I don't have any padding, just heel bone. Pleeeeeese? Just one little piggyback ride? It won't be so bad."

The ocelot rolled its eyes and got down on its knees.

"Yaaaay!" said Brian, and climbed astride the cat.

"Ooh, you're very light," said the ocelot, standing back up. "It must be because you don't have muscles and fat and organs and things."

"See, didn't I tell you it wouldn't be so bad?" said Brian.

"Fine," said the ocelot. "But if you ever tell another ocelot I did this, I will hunt you down."

Ahead of them, Graser privately chuckled at their squabbling.

The red corridor took several twists and turns, and eventually opened onto a large room. It was full of an astonishing amount of crafting materials. Blocks of every sort seemed to be heaped into enormous piles.

"This is very strange," Graser said to himself. "Why is all this crafting material just piled up like this?"

"Drat," said the ocelot. "Still no pool, eh? But I can still smell it. We are getting closer to my fish! We just need to get a little deeper."

A giant voice out of the darkness above said: "THAT CAN BE ARRANGED."

The ocelot jumped so high that Brian fell of its back and clattered to the stone floor. Graser turned his eyes up brighter, searching for the source of the deep, baritone voice. When he searched the upper reaches of the large room, he found it.

Carved into the wall was a huge wolf. It was made of rock, but moved as though it were very much alive. Its piercing blue eyes were made of lapis lazuli. They stared daggers into Graser. (Not literally, of course, but it was still intimidating.)

"Who are you?" Graser asked the stone wolf.

"I AM CALLED THE STONE WOLF," it said.

"Your voice is loud and piercing," Graser said.

"THANK YOU," said the huge wolf. "FLATTERY WILL GET YOU EVERYWHERE. WELL, ALMOST EVERYWHERE. SEE, IT WON'T GET YOU THROUGH THAT DOOR."

With its piercing blue eyes, the wolf indicated a redstone door set into the wall at the far side of the room.

"GETTING THROUGH THERE IS ANOTHER MATTER ENTIRELY."

"Oh yeah?" said Graser.

The Stone Wolf nodded its rocky head. The ceiling of the room shook slightly as it did this.

"And how do I convince you to open the door?" Graser asked.

"YOU HAVE TO SOLVE MY PROBLEM," said the wolf.

"And what's that?" asked Graser, expecting something very complicated.

"I'M HUNGRY," said the wolf.

"Well I hope you don't eat robot crafters or ocelots," Graser said.

"Or skeletons," added Brian. "You wouldn't like us, anyway. No meat."

The Stone Wolf laughed loudly and deeply. Dust fell from the ceiling as it did so.

"What do you like to eat?" asked Graser.

"I'M NOT ALLOWED TO TELL YOU THAT," said the wolf. "ALL I CAN SAY IS THAT THESE BLOCKS HAVE BEEN PLACED HERE AT YOUR DISPOSAL. YOU CAN 'COOK' ANYTHING YOU'D LIKE. NO MATTER WHAT IT IS, I'LL GIVE

IT A TRY. BUT I SHOULD WARN YOU, I DON'T LIKE FOOD THAT TASTES BAD. IT MAKES ME VERY CRANKY."

"Oh," said Graser.

"AND YOU WOULDN'T LIKE ME WHEN I'M CRANKY," said the Stone Wolf. "BELIEVE ME."

"I see," said Graser. "Thank you for the warning. That was most considerate. Please excuse me a moment. My friends and I will see about formulating a menu."

The Stone Wolf nodded to say it understood.

Graser walked to the far corner of the room where he could consult with his companions.

"What do you guys think?" Graser asked.

"How do we feed a wolf that's made out of stone?" asked the ocelot.

"There's got to be something it will like," said Brian. "Everybody likes something, right?"

Graser tried to draw on what knowledge he had of wolves.

"It seems to me that when you want to tame a wolf, you start by feeding it bones," said Graser.

Graser and the ocelot both looked at Brian.

"Hey, don't get any ideas," Brian said. "Besides, that wolf already seems plenty tame to me. He's attached to the wall, after all. He's not going to be running around and chasing people. How much more tame can you get?"

"Relax," said Graser. "I agree that the wolf is already tamed. I'm just. . . what do you call it. . . free associating."

Next, the ocelot piped up.

"The wolves I see tend to eat meat. I wonder if our wolf would be the same."

"Ha," said Brian. "You're the only one made of meat, ocelot. I'm all bone, and Graser's all metal. Looks like you're the one in hot water now!"

"Hey, nobody is feeding anybody to the wolf," Graser said. "Not just because it'd be a lousy thing to do to someone, but also because I don't think it would work. All of this crafting material has been left here as a sort of mystery for me to solve, I think. I need to use it. I'm supposed to craft a version of the Stone Wolf's dinner."

"Craft meat?" said Brian skeptically. "That's about the weirdest thing I ever heard."

"Stick with me, and things are liable to get even weirder," Graser said. "I totally bet we can use the things in this room to craft something the Stone Wolf will like. Let's start by thinking about what kinds of meats there are."

"Ooh, I can help with that," the ocelot said enthusiastically. "That's because I spend most of my free time thinking about different meats. Really, all of my free time. Actually, it would be fair to say that whenever I am not eating meat I am probably thinking about eating some meat. Mostly I think about fish meat. Fish are my favorite. But I don't think wolves eat fish. That's okay, though. Because there are plenty of others."

"So what do you advise, Mr. Meat Expert?" Graser said.

"Well, we've definitely got choices," said the ocelot. "There's cooked pork chops, cooked chicken, cooked rabbit, steak, and cooked mutton. But if you like to eat raw meat—which is probably what wolves are accustomed to—there's raw beef, raw pork chop, raw mutton, raw chicken, and raw rabbit."

By the time the ocelot finished his list, he was breathing hard and licking his lips. Graser was convinced that he really was an expert on the subject.

"Okay," Graser said. "So which of those meats do you think the Stone Wolf would like the most?"

"Raw beef," answered the ocelot.

"That was quick," said Graser. "You sound pretty certain."

"Oh, I definitely am," the ocelot answered. "Beef is probably what a wolf gets to eat the least, so it probably wants it the most. Cows are hard to catch and half the time they're protected by villagers. Managing to get some beef is a challenge, so wolves are likely to want it even more because of that."

"Brian, what do you think?" Graser asked.

"I have no idea," the skeleton said. "Skeletons don't eat meat. Or anything, really. We hunt with our bows and arrows, sure. But that's just for fun."

"It's not very fun for the people being hunted—which half the time are crafters," Graser reminded him.

"No," said Brian through a toothy grin. "But it's plenty of fun for us!"

"Well, okay then," Graser said. "I don't have a better idea. Let's go with raw beef."

"Okay," said the ocelot. "But—err—what exactly do we do?"

"The wolf is made out of stone," reasoned Graser. "So I expect he'd like to eat stone food. Or as close to stone as we can come. Raw beef is red. Let's start by looking through all these crafting materials and figuring out which ones are the right colors."

The trio fanned out and began a slow inventory of the room. There were so many different kinds of crafting material strewn about that the process was rather slow. As they worked, the Stone Wolf looked down at them curiously from its position up on the wall. Once or twice it licked its lips. When they had finished taking stock, the three met again in the center of the room.

"Okay, what did you find?" Graser asked his compatriots.

"I found red sand and red sandstone," said the ocelot. "They were right next to each other. I guess it makes sense that the two would go hand in hand."

"I found hardened clay," said Brian. "It comes in lots of reddish colors. There's quite a variety to choose from."

"And I found a few blocks of red nether brick," said Graser. "That stuff is very rare. I'm impressed they have it at all."

"That's a pretty good collection of red blocks," said the ocelot. "Do you think you'll be able to craft it into the shape of raw steak?"

"Hmm, probably," said Graser. "I wish I had a real piece of raw steak to model it after. But for all the clutter in this room, there doesn't seem to be any food."

An idea suddenly occurred to Graser.

"Ocelot, it sounds like raw meat is always foremost in your mind. Maybe if you could describe raw steak to me in great detail, then I'd know what to craft."

"Okay," said the ocelot. "But I warn you, my stomach may start growling. I can get pretty into it."

"That's fine," Graser said with a laugh. "Just make sure you get the steak parts correct and accurate."

"You won't need to worry about that," the ocelot said.

And Graser didn't.

The ocelot began to describe a tremendous raw steak dinner. He lingered over the exact cut of the meat. He described the marbling on the surface, and the many hues of red and pink that ran through it. He explained that whether you called it steak tartare, or raw beef, or taking a bit of something that had been a cow just a second ago—it was all more or less the same. You were in for deliciousness. You could spread some parsley over the top to make it look fancy if you wanted to, but it wasn't really necessary and did nothing for the taste. You could eat it sitting down or standing up if you were in a hurry. You could eat it with a fork and a knife, with your bare hands, or with your claws if you were an ocelot. You could also have a napkin handy, because afterwards you might have yummy raw steak juice running down your mouth.

As the ocelot spoke, Graser began to craft the various red blocks into a raw steak the right size and shape to be eaten by the Stone Wolf. Graser allowed himself to be inspired by the feline's words. Soon it was as though he could actually see the raw steak forming before him. Glancing up from his work, Graser saw that he wasn't the only one.

"Are you drooling?" Graser asked the skeleton when the ocelot paused from breath.

"I'm as surprised as you are," said Brian. "I've never known myself to be interested in steak before. And plus, I don't even have salivary glands. But this drool is coming from *somewhere.* The ocelot's just so good at describing it. He's made me into a convert, I guess."

Beside them, the ocelot cleared its throat.

"Ahem," it said. "If you don't mind, I'd like to continue. I was just getting to mouthfeel and what it's like when you chew the steak."

"How exciting," said Brian. "Please continue!"

The ocelot did. As it spoke, Graser thought about how to craft his virtual steak so that it would feel right for the big stone wolf that was going to be eating it. He made certain to add bits of hard red nether brick among the softer blocks to give it variation in texture, and to add a couple of white quartz along the edges to simulate fatty bits. After all—as the ocelot emphasized—no raw steak was perfect.

"That's the thing though," the ocelot concluded as Graser finished crafting the enormous rock steak. "It's the fact that no raw steak is perfect that makes them so darn. . .so darn perfect! Each one is different. Each one is special. Each one is . ."

"Stop, stop," Brian said, waving his bony arms in the air. "Please, I can't take it any more. I want a raw steak so bad. I don't even have a stomach, and my stomach's rumbling."

"No, that's me," the ocelot said. "I make myself hungry when I get to talking about food. Well Graser, was it worth all the trouble?"

"I think it was," said Graser standing back to admire his creation.

The skeleton and the ocelot looked on in wonderment.

"Wow," said the ocelot. "It looks just like a real raw steak. Only enormous!"

"If I look at it too long, I start to think maybe it's a steak that got real big. . . or I somehow got shrunk down real small," said Brian. "Either way, it's kind of freaking me out!"

Graser laughed.

"Don't worry," the crafter told his friends. "I don't think it'll be around to tempt you for very long."

Just as these words were out of Graser's mouth, the Stone Wolf perked up from its perch on the other side of the room. Its eyes rolled as it tried to make out what had been created, and its large stone tail twitched with excitement.

"WHAT'S THAT?" the great beast inquired. "CAN YOU MOVE OUT OF THE WAY? I CAN'T SEE."

"You two," help me carry, Graser said.

Using all of his robotic might, Graser picked up one side of the huge raw steak. Brian and the ocelot did their best to hold up the other. But even their combined strengths were not equal to Graser's.

They carefully moved the creation up to the snapping stone lips of the wolf.

"THAT LOOKS DELICIOUS," said the wolf. "GIMMIE."

"Now, now," said Graser. "Where are your manners? Even giant wolves who have the power to open magic doors need to say please."

"PLEEEEEESE," went the Stone Wolf.

"Okay," said Graser.

The wolf opened its enormous jaws. Graser and his companions hoisted the steak high above their heads, just level with the wolf's lower jaw. The wolf's tongue lashed forward like a monkey's prehensile tail and snapped up the raw steak, pulling it forward into the Stone Wolf's mouth.

"OM NOM NOM," went the wolf. "THIS IS THE BEST STEAK I EVER TASTED. IT IS ALSO THE ONLY STEAK I EVER TASTED, BUT STILL. . ."

"Guys, look out," Graser said to his friends. He gazed skyward and lifted his hands over his head as though he were shielding himself from the sun.

"What're you talking ab-" Brian said, but was cut off when an errant piece of stone steak fell from the wolf's mouth and bonked him on the head.

"Ow," Brian said. "That's gonna leave a nick in my skull."

"Maybe we should get out of the splatter zone," said Graser. "Whether they're enormous and made of stone, or regular sized and made of wolf-parts, wolves can be messy eaters."

The three companions moved off and allowed the Stone Wolf to finish its meal. The Stone Wolf relished every bite, chewing slowly, seeming not to want the experience to end. Graser smiled in satisfaction.

"So, did you like your raw steak?" Graser asked. "More importantly, did you like it enough to open the redstone door on the other side of the room?"

Unexpectedly, the wolf let out a loud howl. Graser allowed himself to hope it was a howl of contentment. However, he could see a sudden consternation in the wolf's eyes.

"What is it?" asked Graser.

"I'VE GOT SOMETHING STUCK BETWEEN MY TEETH," said the wolf. "OW! OW! OW! THIS HAS NEVER HAPPENED TO ME BEFORE."

Graser looked closely and saw that there was indeed a sliver of red nether brick wedged between the wolf's lower two front teeth and its gumline.

"Hang on," said Graser. "I bet I can pry that out with a diamond axe. If you hold still, I'll get in there. I've never been a wolf dentist before, but there's a first time for everything."

"NO!" said the wolf.

"What do you mean, 'No'?" said Graser. "Do you want your teeth cleaned or not?"

"YOU'RE RUINING THE. . . THE. . . FANTASY," said the Stone Wolf. "LOOK, I KNOW I'M NOT A REAL WOLF; I'M SOME KIND OF ENCHANTMENT. AND I KNOW I DIDN'T JUST EAT A REAL RAW STEAK. BUT IT'S IMPORTANT FOR ME TO PRETEND THAT I DID. THINGS HAVE TO LOOK JUST SO. JUST RIGHT. HAVING A CRAFTER HANGING OFF MY LOWER JAW LIKE A MOUNTAINEER, HAMMERING AWAY, REMINDS ME THAT I'M MADE OF STONE AND NOT A REAL WOLF. I DON'T LIKE THAT."

"What would you like?" asked Graser.

The Stone Wolf thought for a moment.

"WHAT IF WE USED A TOOTHPICK TO CLEAN MY TEETH?" asked the wolf. "THAT'S WHAT FANCY PEOPLE USE, RIGHT? LIKE IN FIVE-STAR RESTAURANTS? I WANT ONE OF THOSE. IT WOULD BE CLASSY AND APPROPRIATE FOR A WOLF WHO HAS JUST FINISHED A GOURMET STEAK MEAL."

"Well, I guess I could. . ." Graser began.

"AND IT SHOULD BE WINTERGREEN."

"Excuse me?" said Graser.

"THE TOOTHPICK SHOULD BE WINTERGREEN. WHAT? HAVEN'T YOU EVER HEARD OF A WINTERGREEN TOOTHPICK? THAT'S TOTALLY A THING. ESPECIALLY AMONG FANCY PEOPLE."

"But. . ." said Graser.

"NO BUTS. YOU NEED TO MAKE ME A WINTERGREEN TOOTHPICK IF YOU WANT ME TO OPEN THE REDSTONE DOOR. SORRY, BUT I'M CHANGING THE AGREEMENT. THAT'S WHAT YOU HAVE TO DO NOW."

Graser threw up his robotic hands and began to pace around the room. How was he going to make a toothpick big enough for a giant wolf? Moreover, how was he going to make it 'wintergreen' . . . whatever that was? Graser had never heard of a wintergreen tree or a wintergreen bush. It sounded like a made up flavor concocted by food companies.

Graser turned to his traveling companions.

"Do you two have any ideas for this?" he asked. "There's bound to be enough wooden crafting components in this room to make a big toothpick. But I'm less familiar with how to make something wintergreen."

"It does sound like a classy flavor," opined Brian, "but also like you don't know exactly what it is. Maybe that's what makes it classy!"

"When I try to picture something wintergreen, I think of something that's not really green," said the ocelot. "It's more blue-green. And then its cold and icy. That's where you get the winter part."

Something clicked inside of Graser's head. (Probably it was a gear or a sprocket—seeing as how he was an actual mechanical robot—but it also made him realize something he hadn't thought of before.)

"Hold on," said Graser. "Ocelot, what did you just say?"

"Err. . . cold and icy, and that's where the winter part comes from. . . I think. . .," the ocelot replied.

Graser reached into his inventory and took out the blue ice spike that the old man had given him as a gift. True to the old man's conjectures, it had not melted at all. It seemed to be supernaturally possessed with the spirit of ice and snow.

"Ooh," said the ocelot. "Pretty!"

"What's that?" said Brian, marveling at the long, blue spike. "It doesn't look quite like anything I've seen before, but it definitely gives me a 'winter' sort of vibe."

"An old man gave it to me near the start of my journey," Graser said. "It's made of winter ice and seems to be enchanted. And I think it might make the perfect tip of a wintergreen toothpick."

Graser set about to his work. He found several blocks of wood and fashioned them into a single wooden pole that would be long enough to reach the mouth of the Stone Wolf. Next he took some twine and tied the blue ice spike to the tip of the pole. He made sure to tie it very tightly so it didn't become dislodged during the cleaning.

The blue ice spike sparkled in the light from Graser's eyes, almost as if it knew it had been made for this purpose.

"Here you go," Graser said to the Stone Wolf after he had finished the toothpick. "I've got a nice wintergreen toothpick for you. Open up and say 'Ahhhhh.'"

"NO!" said the Stone Wolf, sounding horrified. "I HAVE DO USE THE TOOTHPICK MYSELF. OTHERWISE, PEOPLE WILL THINK I'M A LITTLE BABY."

"But how are you going to hold the toothpick?" Graser asked. "Your wolf-hands don't even have opposable thumbs."

"I GUESS YOU'RE RIGHT," the wolf said, glancing down at itself. "OKAY, YOU DO IT. BUT PLEASE, DON'T TELL ANYONE ABOUT IT."

"I promise it will be our little secret

Using the enormous toothpick, Graser dislodged the piece of 'steak' between the Stone Wolf's teeth. It clattered to the floor.

"WOW," said the Stone Wolf. "THAT'S MUCH BETTER. MY TEETH FEEL TOTALLY AWESOME. PLUS, I FEEL CLASSY BECAUSE THEY GOT CLEANED WITH A WINTERGREEN TOOTHPICK."

"I'd say we've more than fulfilled our side of this bargain," Graser asserted boldly.

"I'D SAY YOU HAVE TOO," said the Stone Wolf. "THANK YOU."

The creature looked in the direction of the redstone door on the far side of the room. It suddenly popped open, revealing a dark corridor beyond. The Stone Wolf smiled.

"Thank you," said Graser. "Pleasure doing business. So to speak."

"THE PLEASURE HAS BEEN ALL MINE," the Stone Wolf said politely. "THAT STEAK WAS DELICIOUS!"

With that, Graser, Brian, and the ocelot made their way through the redstone door and into the corridor beyond, leaving the satisfied Stone Wolf behind.

The corridor was long and windy. Graser had no idea how long it would go on for. He was optimistic that they might soon encounter the ocelot's stockpile of fish—if, indeed, it still existed—because the floor seemed to slope downwards ever so slightly. Water, also, flowed downward. They would soon, Graser calculated, be moving underground. Whether the castle had dungeons, or other things, in its gloomy depths was something Graser didn't yet know. But he was prepared to find out. He was prepared to do anything necessary to solve the castle's mysteries.

As if reading his thoughts, the ocelot said: "You must be feeling good, eh?"

"Oh?" said Graser.

The ocelot nodded.

"Yeah," the ocelot clarified. "We're getting deeper into the castle. Soon you're liable to learn who your creator was. Or is. Are they even still alive?"

Graser thought for a moment.

"I guess I don't know," Graser said. "There's a whole lot I don't know. But the story of my creator has always been the biggest question I had. I never thought I'd have the chance to answer it. Now that I have that chance, I'm determined to do my best."

"You must have had some *guesses* about who created you, right?" said Brian.

"Not really," Graser told the skeleton. "It's always been a bit of a black box."

"I can relate," Brian said. "Skeletons don't have many guesses about who we were, either. Most skeletons never bother trying to figure it out. We have more important things to do. Same goes for zombies. We know it's just a waste of time trying to find out who you were before you got reanimated. Like, if you go up to a villager and ask him: 'Hey, do I look like someone you knew before he got reanimated as a skeleton or zombie?' That villager's not going to be helpful. That villager's just going to run away screaming."

"Yeah," said Graser. "But that's because most of the time you try to shoot villagers with arrows or—in the case of zombies—bite them to death."

"Well, I mean. . . Yeah. I suppose you're right."

"Imagine how you would feel if it was possible to find out who you had been and where you had come from," Graser said to the skeleton. "I know it's not possible, but just pretend that somehow it was. You'd be curious, right?"

Brian thought for a moment.

"Perhaps I would be just the teensiest bit curious," Brian allowed.

"Then maybe you can guess how I'm feeling at the moment," Graser said. "I want to do well and solve all of these mysteries and challenges. But what if I don't? Is my creator watching? Is he or she waiting for me in the bowels of the castle?"

"Like maybe in a pool filled with all my yummy fish?" conjectured the ocelot.

"Yeah, maybe," said Graser with a grin. "There's just a lot I don't know about how this is going to go down. I feel a bit anxious and confused, to be honest."

"Well you better suck it up and prepare yourself," said the ocelot, "because I see another room up ahead."

The ocelot was right. Several yards up the corridor they discovered a large square room of stone bricks. The room was almost entirely empty. Into the far wall of the room were set two redstone doors. To the side of the doors was a polished granite pillar, about the height of a person. The top of it had been filed down, shaping it into a kind of lectern. Leaning against the lectern was a very tired looking zombie.

"Zzzzzz," went the zombie.

Graser, the ocelot, and Brian peered into this strange room from the doorway.

"Do you know that zombie?" Graser asked. "I mean, apparently you both work here at the castle."

Brian shook his skull.

"No. Never seen him before in my life."

"Do you think it's some kind of trap?" said the ocelot. "A sleeping zombie and two doors. It seems, I dunno, a little suspicious."

"I've seen more suspicious things," Graser said stepping forward bravely into the room.

At the sound of Graser's diamond boots on the hard stone floor, the zombie snored itself away.

"That's some bad sleep apnea," the ocelot observed. "He should really get that checked out."

"Shh," said Graser to the ocelot.

They stepped up to the podium. The zombie straightened itself, as though preparing to receive them. It had a moldy green face like most zombies, and its clothing had rotted away in patches. It seemed very old and very smelly. Graser hoped they would not have to be near it for very long.

"Which one of you is Graser?" the zombie moaned.

Graser lifted a finger.

"Very well," said the zombie. "I am here to administer a test to you. Now listen carefully. Before you are two doors. Behind both of them are dark corridors. One of the corridors leads to the final mystery in the center of the castle. The other leads to a pit."

"Oh," said Graser. "A pit doesn't sound very nice."

"Wait," said the zombie. "It gets worse."

"Ooh, I know," said the ocelot. "It's filled with pointy knives, right? Pits are always filled with pointy knives."

"Or what about acid," said Brian. "Even if you're a skeleton, you have to be worried about acid. It can melt you down into nothing, even if you're just bones."

"What about lava?" said the ocelot. "Lava could do that too."

Graser glowered at his companions to say they should be quiet.

"Do you want him to tell us or not?" Graser said grumpily.

The ocelot and skeleton silently hung their heads.

"Please continue," Graser said to the zombie.

"Thanks," the zombie said. "The pit is full of. . .seeds."

Though Graser was made of metal, everyone in the room would have sworn that he turned slightly pale.

"Seeds. . ." said Graser. "Why'd it have to be seeds?"

The ocelot screwed up its face, as though concerned it was not hearing things right.

"Seeds? Like the ones you plan it the ground and then trees happen? What's the big deal with them? They're too small to hurt you. I imagine that falling into a pit of them might actually be a good bit of fun. You could swim around in them. And if you got hungry, you could just take a bite! Seeds are delicious."

"I. . .just don't like seeds," Graser said. "They really upset me. Don't ask me why."

Although Graser felt slightly faint at the prospect of seeds in his future, one thing about it did make him feel better. Namely, it was an aspect of the castle tailored precisely to him. The prior problems were things that anybody could have engaged with and solved. But a challenge with seeds as a possible consequence? That had been designed with *Graser in mind.* That made him feel like someone was indeed watching him. Maybe someone like his creator.

Graser looked back at the zombie. Its undead lips curled into a particularly evil smile.

"They *told* me you might have this reaction," the zombie said. "I hardly believed it. But there you go."

"Hey," said the ocelot. "Be nice to Graser. Do you even know who you're talking to? He's a master crafter and a really cool robot. And you're just. . . just. . . What are you, anyway?"

"I am called the Answerer," the zombie said. "You may be wondering how you are supposed to choose between the two doors. Well. . . You are allowed to ask me any question that you like. It is my function as the Answerer to provide a response. When you are satisfied that you have learned all that you can from my responses, you should pick a door and proceed."

Graser, the ocelot, and Brian all looked at one another. This challenge seemed like it might be the easiest they had encountered so far.

"This should be no problem," said the ocelot to Graser. "Just ask him which door leads to where we want to go. Ooh, and also, while you're at it, as him which one leads to my fish. I know they're around here somewhere."

Graser suspected there might be more to it than that, but thought the ocelot's suggestion might be a good place to start.

"Okay," said Graser, turning back to the zombie. "Which one of these doors leads to the final mystery at the center of the castle, where we want to go? Is it the right one, or the left one?"

"Oh it is *definitely* the door on the left," said the Answerer. "No question about it. Open that door, and behind it is a pathway leading directly to where you want to go. And *not* to any nasty, scary seeds."

The ocelot cleared its throat.

"Oh yeah," Graser said. "And which one leads to the ocelot's pool of fish."

"That's also the left door," the Answerer said.

The ocelot smiled.

"See, that wasn't so hard," said the ocelot. It began making for the door on the left. The Answerer watched it with a grin. Graser reached out and grabbed the ocelot's shoulder before it was out of arm's reach.

"Not so fast," Graser said.

He turned back to the zombie.

"One more question," Graser said to the Answerer. "Do you tell the truth?"

The zombie did not speak for a moment.

The ocelot said: "Ooh, so he's a liar, eh?"

"Wait," said the zombie. "I never said I was a liar."

"But do you always tell the truth then?" Graser pressed.

"I mean. . . I tell the truth about *most* things," said the zombie.

The ocelot was incensed. Graser was now holding him back to prevent him attacking the zombie.

"They shouldn't even call you 'the Answerer,'" the ocelot said. "They should just call you the big fat fibber!"

"Settle down, ocelot," Graser said. "We've got to figure out when he is lying and when he is telling the truth. I think this is part of the mystery."

"Oh," said the ocelot, becoming slightly less rambunctious. "Okay. But I still think it's bad that he's a fibber. Especially about something so serious as the location of all my delicious fish."

"When do you tell the truth, and when do you lie?" Graser asked the zombie.

"I tell the truth when I feel like it," the zombie said with a shrug.

"Are you feeling like it right now?" Graser pressed.

"Yes," said the zombie. "Although. . . I could be lying about that."

Brian spoke up.

"This guy is hopeless. We'll never know when he's telling the truth or lying. We might as well flip a coin to decide which door to take."

"Not necessarily," said Graser. "I have a feeling that if we're very careful, we can still get to the bottom of this."

Graser knew there had to be a way to get the Answerer to slip up and tell them the true way to go. Graser knew how hard it could be to conceal a lie, or to keep a lie straight. He decided that if he asked the Answerer enough questions, it would be likely to betray itself.

Graser stepped back up to the zombie who waited behind its podium.

"Tell me, am I a robot?" Graser asked.

"Huh?" said the zombie. "Is this some sort of joke? You're supposed to ask me what tunnel to take, but now you're getting all metaphysical?"

"What?" Graser said innocently. "I'm just asking a simple question. Am I a robot? Do I have mechanical parts and glowing red eyes and dark metal skin?"

"Well. . . yes," said the Answerer. "Anybody can see that."

"Are you as certain about my being a robot as you are about which door holds the seeds, and which the way forward?"

"I. . . I. . ." the zombie stammered. "I know you're a robot, and I know which door goes where. Don't try to trick me, Graser. I'm too clever."

"I wouldn't dream of doing that," Graser said innocently. "As you can see, I'm just trying to get my facts straight."

"Okay then," said the zombie. "But I'm warning you. No tricks."

"Of course not," said Graser. "I'm just finding out about you. I've never met an Answerer before. I want to learn all about you, and all the interesting things you know."

The zombie seemed a little flattered, and smiled at Graser. Graser had learned you could get a lot from a person by making them feel important.

"I've also never been in a room with a floor of such beautiful blue prismarine," Graser said.

The zombie lifted an eyebrow. (True, it had only one eyebrow because the other had long since rotted away, but it sure knew how to make use of the one it still had.)

"I'd say the floor of this room is stone brick," said the Answerer. "Where are you coming from with this blue prismarine angle?"

Graser winked at his compatriots. They knew what to do.

"Oh, this floor is definitely blue prismarine," said the ocelot.

"If you think it's not blue prismarine, then it makes me wonder about how much of the Overworld you've seen," said Brian. "Like, maybe you've just never seen blue prismarine before. What a pity. Some people are so inexperienced."

This was more than the zombie could take.

"I *do* know what blue prismarine is!" the zombie shouted. "The floor of this room is stone brick! Graser is a robot! And the way to the center of this castle is the door on the right!"

Everyone froze.

"*I mean the left*!!!" the zombie corrected itself. "You should take the door on the left! That's what I was supposed to be telling you!"

"Thank you," said Graser. "That was all I needed to know."

He began to stride confidently toward the door on the right. The ocelot and the skeleton followed after him. Graser put his hand on the doorknob.

"This is your fault!" said the Answerer. "You confused me! You cheated somehow!"

Graser ignored the zombie and opened the door on the right. Beyond it was a jet black corridor. He strode down it with no hesitation, his glowing red eyes lighting the way. The ocelot and the skeleton followed. Graser could hear the protestations of the zombie getting further and further away.

"Say," said the ocelot. "How did you know to do that?"

"I find that people like to lie, but they don't like being lied to," Graser said. "When you tell someone a whole bunch of lies, they suddenly become a real evangelist for the truth. Even if it runs contrary to their purposes, like it did for that zombie."

"What do you think we're going to find at the end of this tunnel?" the ocelot asked.

"Well, I hope not seeds, because then I was wrong about everything," Graser said with a chuckle. "Actually, I have a feeling there will be at least one more test."

There was.

They reached a large iron door at the end of the hallway. It had two giant iron handles. Graser gripped both of them at the same time, and prepared to throw them wide.

"If a whole bunch of seeds spill out all over me, I'm going to be really, really, annoyed," Graser said.

"I still don't see why seeds are such a big deal," the ocelot whispered to the skeleton.

Graser shut his eyes tight and opened the doors.

There was no cascade of seeds. At least not that Graser could hear. Upon opening his eyes, Graser saw a staircase leading down to the darkness below. There was also the unmistakable smell of fresh water. Abruptly, Graser felt himself being hit in the spot where a human would have a kidney (but Graser just had gears and bolts) as the ocelot pushed past and stormed down the stairs.

"Outta my way," cried the ocelot. "I smell fish!"

Graser and Brian slowly followed in the ocelot's steps. As he made his way down the steps, Graser heard a splashing sound that sounded very much like an ocelot jumping into a pool of water. As Graser and Brian descended the staircase and looked around the room below, that was exactly what they found.

"My fish!" the ocelot cried. "My beautiful, wonderful fish! They're all here."

The chamber seemed a kind of basement, with the circular pool (containing, yes, all the ocelot's fish) in the center of the room. The ocelot frolicked in the water happily, splashing this way and that. Yet Graser was more interested in a more conventional feature of the room. Against the far wall was a single wood door. Next to it was a small stand. Upon that stand was a placard with a message written upon it. The message was written in the same hand as the note in the book that had been left in front of Graser's palace.

Graser glanced over and saw the ocelot fanning out a handful of multicolored fish in its pawns, the way a dealer might fan a deck of cards. The fish squirmed to escape, but the ocelot held them fast. Graser had never seen an ocelot look so pleased.

"See!" the ocelot said. "I told you they built this castle right over my storage pool. These are all the best looking, tastiest fish I ever caught. Now I'll need to decide if I try to transport them to another pool. . . or if I simply eat them all in one sitting. Either way, it's a good problem to have."

Graser ignored the ocelot. He didn't mean to be rude, but he had his own concerns. Was the mystery of his creation about to be revealed? Trembling with excitement, Graser approached the placard and began to read.

Opening this door requires a special key.
A master crafter would have no problem opening it.
Graser is a master crafter.
If he succeeds, beyond lies the answer to all his questions.

Graser began to examine the door more closely. It was not entirely made from wood. It had a metal handle and a keyhole carved from solid diamond. On the ground near the door were a few blocks that someone seemed to have left behind in rush. Perhaps the people who had built the door had left them there after the construction. Or perhaps there was another explanation.

Graser read the placard a second time, then a third. He wanted to be very certain he understood the rules of this challenge. From what he could tell, it might be his last.

After a few moments, the ocelot wandered over from the pool, leaving wet footprints in the stone brick floor. It was happily chomping on a sunfish, and had placed another behind its ear for later. The ocelot chewed thoughtfully.

"What're you supposed to do here, then?" it asked.

"I just have to open the door," Graser replied. "Apparently, it requires a key."

"Have you *tried* it without a key?" asked the ocelot. It approached the door, wiped the fish from its paws, and gave a hard tug on the knob. No dice.

"Oh," it said. "I think maybe you *do* need a key." Graser nodded.

"I'll leave this to the expert," the ocelot continued with a shrug, "but tell me if I can assist you somehow. I would never have found my pool of fish again if you hadn't come along. I owe you big time!"

"No problem," said Graser.

Graser began to investigate the blocks at his feet. They looked haphazard and forgotten, but Graser wondered if that might not be a red herring intended to throw him off the correct path. He studied the blocks carefully.

One was stone brick. There was a polished andesite and a polished diorite. There was a chiseled sandstone block and a block of oak wood. And three blocks of redstone.

"Hmm," Graser said. "This is very strange."

"What is?" said the ocelot between chews. (It had already moved on to the fish behind its ear.)

"These crafting materials are all wrong," Graser said. "I don't believe you could make a key out of them. Moreover, they're weak compared to diamond. If you put a key crafted from weak material into a diamond lock, it would break, and that would just jam the lock. Diamond's very hard, you see. About the hardest material there is."

The ocelot chewed thoughtfully.

"Well, it doesn't say you have to craft a key," the ocelot said. "It just says you shouldn't have any problem opening the door. It's sort of implied but. . . I dunno. It certainly doesn't say you have to use those inferior blocks on the floor, does it?"

Graser realized the ocelot was right. It didn't.

"Hmm," Graser said. "The placard says I shouldn't have any trouble opening the door. But it says the door needs a key."

"Maybe the key is not necessarily in this room?" said the ocelot. "Ooh, I know. Maybe it's at the bottom of my pool of yummy fish. I think I should go check if it's there, just to be sure."

This gave Graser an idea.

"I think maybe I know how to open the door," Graser said. "And I'm afraid it doesn't have anything to do with your pool of fish."

Graser reached inside his inventory and pulled out a key.

"When I was walking here, I helped some villagers who had been overrun by sledding fanatics," Graser said. "They gave me this key as a token of their appreciation. Apparently, it can open lots of doors. I wonder if it can open this one."

"But. . . but. . ." stammered the ocelot. "That seems weird. The people who build this castle and wrote this note for you, they couldn't have known you'd stop along the journey here and help some villagers, right? That wasn't part of the test, was it?"

Graser shrugged.

"That's one of the odd things about tests," Graser said. "Sometimes you don't even know when you're taking them."

Graser approached the door and slid the villagers' key into the lock. As if by magic, it seemed to fit perfectly.

"Nice," Graser said with a grin.

Suddenly, from out of the darkest corner of the room, an alarmed voice cried: "Wait!"

Graser and the ocelot looked. It was Brian. He looked very upset. (Though his skull had no features, the arrangement still managed to comport the fact that he was quite unhappy about the situation.)

"Brian," Graser said in confusion. "I was wondering where you'd got off to."

"I don't think you should open that door," Brian said firmly.

"No?" asked Graser. "Why not? As you can see, my key fits perfectly."

"I think. . ." Brian said struggling to find the right words. "I think there's something I ought to tell you."

"What?" Graser said. He was beginning to feel a little cross with Brian. Why was the skeleton interrupting him like this, especially as he got so close to his moment of truth?

"Okay. . .but please don't be mad at me," Brian began. "Promise you won't be mad at me?"

"I can't promise that," Graser said. "First I have to hear what you're going to say."

Brian sighed.

"I didn't mean to deceive you," Brian said. "It's just that you seemed like such a nice robot. And then the ocelot was friendly too—if a little annoying—and he seemed to really want his fish. So I thought maybe if I played along I could be friends with you. You both seem like cool guys. And then the ocelot might get his fish and. . . and. . . and I guess I didn't really think through the rest of it."

"What?" said Graser. "What's going on? What aren't you telling us?"

The ocelot, chewing yet another fish, walked over to Brian aggressively.

"Yeah," it said. "Spill the beans."

Brian hung his skull. He was clearly ashamed about this next part of his story, whatever it might be.

"This is all a trick to steal your palace," the skeleton said to Graser. "For years, the zombies and skeletons have been trying to find a way into your palace. It's about the best structure in the Overworld. We really want to get inside. But it's so hard to do. Your doors have been too tricky for our best, sneakiest locksmiths who have come to try your locks in the middle of the night. And also, when you're home and you notice us, you have a habit of bonking us on the head with diamond swords when we come too close."

"I don't understand," said Graser. "My palace is very far away. I took a long journey from it just to get here."

"That was the plan!" said Brian. "The skeletons and the zombies got together to cooperate on stealing your castle. We knew you were too tough for us to ever take it by force. We understood we would have to use trickery. We were the ones who wrote that note in the book, saying you should go on this quest."

"You have very good handwriting, considering you're undead," Graser observed.

"We worked together to built Redstone Castle way out here on the edge of the Overworld, and we built these challenges inside—but it was all to distract you and waste your time," continued Brian. "We guessed that trying to find out who your creator would be a good motivator. It looks like we were right. But you're going far too fast. We thought it would take you much longer to solve all these challenges. And this last one is supposed to be unsolvable. That door has a magic diamond lock that is supposed to break any key."

"Good thing I have this key that can open any door," Graser said.

"But you're a nice guy, and I'm starting to think that the zombie and skeleton leadership were lying to us when they said you were a bad person who deserved to have his palace stolen," Brian said. "Now that I've met you, I think you're actually a very nice person."

"Thank you," said Graser. "That's very kind. Now I have a question—although I think I know the answer. While I've been on the long journey, and trying to solve the mysteries of this castle. . .?"

"A horde of zombies and skeletons have been trying to break into your palace," Brian confirmed. "I'm sorry."

As if to confirm that Brian's tale was true, Graser turned the key that the villagers had made for him. For a moment the diamond lock resisted, but eventually it gave way. Then Graser threw open the door. There was only a brick wall behind it.

"I know I should be disappointed—because I was hoping to find out who created me—but right now I'm just surprised and annoyed," said Graser. "But if what you've said about me getting through these challenges more quickly than expected is true, then maybe there's still time for me to get back home and stop the zombies and skeletons before they break into my house."

Graser turned resolutely toward the staircase, preparing to leave the way they had come.

"Hang on a second," cried the ocelot. "I'm coming with you. You helped me get back to my pool of fish after these annoying undead built a castle right on top of it. I never would have done that, otherwise. I'm in debt to you. I'll help you in any way I can."

"Thank you," said Graser.

"And the first way I'll help you is by telling you there's a much faster way out of here," said the ocelot. "There's a plug at the bottom of my pool. If I pull it, we can crawl down the drain pipe. It empties out way over in the next biome."

"There was a pipe leading to your pool the whole time?" said Graser. "Why didn't you crawl up it before?"

"Because if you open it, it drains the pool," said the ocelot.

"And that's okay to do now?" wondered Graser.

"Yes," said the ocelot, "because—burp!—I've eaten all the fish."

It gestured to the side of the pool. There was a pile of fish skeletons heaped beside it. And, now that Graser looked closely, the ocelot's belly looked more than slightly swollen.

"That sounds like a good plan," said Graser. "Pull out the plug and drain the pool."

The ocelot hopped into the water and began to dive down to the bottom.

"Can I come too?" said Brian. "I feel so awful about having been a part of this ploy. I want to make up for it."

"You really want to come with me?" Graser asked.

"Yes," said Brian. "Maybe I can be useful. I'm good at shooting a bow, and plus I speak skeleton."

"Err, don't skeletons just speak the same language as everybody else?" Graser asked.

"Yeah," said Brian. "Only words are much bonier when we say them."

Graser smirked.

"Okay, you can come along," Graser told him. "But this had better not be yet another ploy. . .like one designed to smuggle a skeleton into my palace on the pretense of helping me, for example."

"I promise it's not," said Brian. "I'm done with ploys. I'm going to be totally honest with people from now on!"

"I think that's a good policy to live by," said Graser. "I'm proud of you, Brian."

Suddenly, a very wet ocelot appeared beside them.

"Okay," it said. "Pool's drained. Are you guys ready to go?"

They were.

At the bottom of the ocelot's pool was indeed a drain. It was just big enough for them to shimmy through. Beyond was a series of dark drainage tunnels. They were hot and wet and mucky. The floor beneath their feet had been turned to mud by the draining water from the pool.

"Good thing your eyes light up," said the ocelot, "because I don't think a torch would burn down here. It's far too humid. The moisture in the air would put it right out."

"Maybe so," said Graser. "How long will we be in this drain tunnel, anyway?"

"It runs all the way to the next biome," said the ocelot. "So I guess a while."

"Does it get any wider along the way?" Graser asked, bumping his head on the roof of the tunnel. "Or taller?"

"Sorry," said the ocelot. "It's like this pretty much the entire time. But hey, we're still going much faster than we otherwise would be, especially if we had to climb all the way back through that castle."

"I hope you're right about that," said Graser.

They followed along the tunnel until they reached an opening set into the side of a hill. It was a rather *extreme* hill, Graser realized quite quickly. And so were the hills stretching into the distance beyond it.

"I don't believe it," Graser said. "The Hills of Extreme Sledding. You've done it!"

"You're welcome," said the ocelot. "I never though when I dug this drainage tunnel that it'd come in so handy one day."

Graser looked out into the biome. It was still filled with people on sleds, but it looked as though quite a few of them were now using sleds with feathery tops and emerald-studded undersides.

"That didn't take long," Graser said to himself. "I guess a good idea catches on quickly."

Graser led his band down from the side of the hill to the valley below. They walked across the biome and watched the sledders cavorting on the tops of the hills around them, dipping up and down in the noonday sun. Suddenly, Graser noticed a figure in the distance who seemed to be waving. He was the size and shape of a villager. He looked somehow, familiar, but Graser could not quite place him.

Graser elected to make a very slight detour in order to investigate.

As the figure came into view, Graser realized it was the famer. However, the man was changed. He wore the finest farming overalls Graser had ever seen, and carried a straw hat that appeared to have been spun from pure gold.

"Graser!" the farmer said happily. He ran up and gave the black robot a big hug around the shoulders.

"You're certainly looking prosperous," Graser said. "That didn't take long. How long has it been since I was here last? Less than a day, surely."

"You're right," said the farmer. "It happened so fast I could hardly believe it. . .but the important thing is, it happened! Our economy has been totally transformed. Everybody in the Overworld wants our sleds. The village has made me vice president in charge of emerald acquisition. It a really big job. And the sledders have stopped scavenging entirely. Our village looks even more beautiful that it did when it was first built!"

"I'm glad to see things have worked out so well," Graser told the farmer. "I'm afraid I can't stay to celebrate. I've got a problem of my own, as it happens. A bunch of zombies and skeletons have played a trick on me by sending me on a fake errand. Now they're trying to break into my palace while I'm not there. I've got to hurry home and stop them."

"Hmm," said the farmer. "I wish I knew of any ways to help you get there faster, but I don't. These sleds are very good for going up and down, but not overland— though you probably knew that already."

"Yes, I did," said Graser.

"I won't keep you then," said the farmer. "Best of luck on your journey. If you ever pass this way again, always know that you have our eternal gratitude."

"Thank you," said Graser, and hurried on his way.

Graser, Brian, and the ocelot passed through the Hills of Extreme Sledding until they began to wane and become much smaller.

"They should call these the bunny hills of wimpy sledding," quipped the ocelot.

"I dunno," said Brian. "They still look pretty exciting to me. If only we had time to stop and have a sled."

"Don't get any ideas," said Graser. "We can sled all we want . . . *after* we save my palace."

Graser and his group continued on, and an icy wind began to blow. In the distance they could see snow falling from the sky, and white rabbits with tiny pink eyes frolicking in the underbrush. The horizon was filled with ice spikes that were tall, thick, and slightly blue.

"It's the Blue Ice Plains Spikes biome," Graser reported. "It won't be much further now."

"So *this* is where you found a wintergreen toothpick big enough for that Stone Wolf," said the ocelot. "I was wondering about that."

They moved deeper into the biome. Ice crystals began to cover them. Snowflakes drifted down lazily from the sky.

"Do you think we have time to stop and catch a rabbit?" the ocelot asked. "They look delicious."

"First of all, they look like pairs of floating red eyes out here," Graser said. "Second of all, no, I'm afraid we need to keep moving. Third, aren't you supposed to be full of fish now?"

The ocelot looked chastened.

"Oh, I am," it said. "But eating all those fish sort of turned on my desire to eat things. I'm suddenly very hungry all the time."

"Well hang in there just a little bit longer," Graser said. "When we reach my palace, I'll prepare a four-star feast for you. Providing the place hasn't been totally sacked by zombies and skeletons, that is."

They continued through the Blue Ice Plains Spikes biome and soon reached the edge of the desert. Graser looked thoughtfully at the sand spreading out before him. He stopped and hesitated.

"What's the matter?" said the ocelot.

Graser put a metal hand up to his glowing red eyes to cut the glare from the sun. He was looking carefully across the sandy hills, scrutinizing each dune. He looked at them for a long time.

"Hey, I'm talking to you," said the ocelot.

"Yes," I hear you," said Graser. "I'm looking for any sign of the zombies or skeletons. If they were gathering to attack my palace as soon as I left it, they must have crossed this desert at some point. But I can't see any of their tracks."

Brian stepped forward.

"Actually, I think I can help explain that," he said. "When skeletons walk across the desert, our footbones are so tiny that they don't make much of a mark in the sand. If you see the footprints, you might mistake them for a trail left by a small animal or a bird."

"Hmm," said Graser. "Now that you mention it, I *do* see a lot of tiny trails left by birds."

"And as to the zombies," said Brian. "When they want to conceal their numbers, they always walk exactly in the footsteps of the zombie who walked in front of them. Instead of lots of footprint trails—which is what you might be looking for—they leave one set of footprints. The only thing remarkable about it is the set will be deep, because so many zombies have walked there."

"There *is* a single set of tracks running across the desert," Graser said. "And they are very deep looking. I thought maybe they were my own tracks from earlier, when I cross the desert going the other way."

"You should go and have a look at them," Brian said.

Graser agreed, and they trekked to the set of heavy footprints just visible along the horizon. When they were five or ten yards away, Graser looked back to compare his own prints with this other set. They were indeed very different. Also, vitally, the other set of heavy prints pointed toward his palace, not away."

"This is definitely the zombies," Brian said. "They were probably hiding somewhere, and they crossed as soon as you entered Redstone Castle."

"In that case, they don't really have that much of a head start," said Graser. "Maybe we can still catch them before they breach my defenses."

"Defenses?" said Brian.

"You'll see," answered Graser.

They hurried across the desert and reached the biomes directly surrounding Graser's palace. Soon, they encountered the small village closest to where Graser lived. It was clear that the zombies and skeletons had been through here, and that they had abandoned measures to conceal their presence. The village was ruined! The crops were trampled, the animals had been eaten, and the buildings were in ruins. There were zombie footprints—and skeleton boneprints—everywhere.

The village looked like a ghost town.

"This is awful," said Graser. "Those skeletons and zombies are going to pay."

"Where are all the villagers?" asked the ocelot.

"They've run away if they had any sense," Graser answered. "That is to say, I *hope* they've run away..."

All three swallowed hard, not wanting to imagine the alternative.

They could now see the uppermost towers of Graser's palace in the distance. They hurried toward it. As they got closer, they began to detect a foul smell in the air. It was rotting flesh mixed with old bones that had been in the ground for a very long time. The ocelot—the only member of the party with a proper flesh-and-blood nose—turned it up in disgust.

As they grew closer still, the air became dusty. It was as though the attacking armies had kicked up the dirt in their haste to reach the palace, and some of it still hung in the air. Then they encountered a zombie's hand lying on the trail before them. Then they encountered a foot. Then a second foot.

"The zombies got excited when they got this close," Graser deduced. "They started running, and literally ran themselves apart. . . at least in a few cases."

"Zombies shouldn't run," said Brian. "As a skeleton, I should know. Any zombie who runs is asking for whatever he gets."

This made Graser laugh.

Then they continued forward and crested a hill near the crafting grounds in front of the castle. The sight on the other side of it was startling. There was Graser's palace—immense, towering, and immaculately crafted. But around it were zombies and skeletons of every size and shape. The air was thick with the noises they made— odd moans and strange clicks. There had to be hundreds and hundreds of them. They did not seem to be attacking the castle in any proper sense, but instead hurrying to and fro carrying materials. They appeared to be building something. It was not immediately clear what it might be, but they were constructing it a few yards out from the castle door. In front of their construction was a hole that radiated out the healthy glow of fire or lava.

"What in the Overworld is this?" the ocelot whispered.

"Yeah," said Brian. "What's happening?"

"Exactly what's supposed to happen," Graser said with a mysterious smile. "My palace defenses are working. I couldn't be more pleased."

"Pleased?" asked Brian. "What are you talking about?"

"There's a moat of lava surrounding my palace," Graser told them. "It's just that most of the time nobody knows its there. It's covered by a very thin layer of polished granite blocks that I've hammered to the point they're nearly broken. Then that's covered with dirt. When you or I—or any normal visitor coming to my palace—walks across it, it doesn't break. But when an army of people I don't like—for example, zombies or skeletons—try to walk across it together. . . Well, you see what happens."

"I do!" said Brian. "So the skeletons have realized that the ground around the palace can crumble into lava. And so they're building a bridge over it?"

"Looks like it to me," Graser said. "The lava moat is doing just what it's supposed to do. It won't keep a clever enemy away from my palace for too long, but it will certainly slow them down. Now that these undead have had to stop and deal with this, we can think about how we're going to defeat them."

"Ooh, and how are we going to do that?" the ocelot said enthusiastically. "Does it involve you and Brian going into battle armed to the teeth and wearing shining diamond armor—while I hide underneath a bush somewhere—because that sounds like the best course of action to me."

"Don't worry," said Graser. "I know ocelots don't have that many hearts of health. I wouldn't ask you to go into combat against hundreds of skeletons and zombies. I don't think I'd ask that of *myself*, now that you mention it."

"Whew," said the ocelot, looking relieved.

Then Graser said: "But Brian here, on the other hand…"

The skeleton looked petrified.

"What?" said Brian. "You're not thinking of sending *me* up against that horde, are you?"

"Just listen," said Graser, leaning over to whisper confidentially into Brian's ear-hole. "I have a plan."

Moments later, Brian emerged from the cover of the hillside and began striding down toward the mass of skeletons and zombies still working feverishly to construct a bridge over Graser's lava moat. Only once did he stop and hesitate.

"Are you absolutely *sure* about this?" he whispered back to the hill behind him, his pace slackening.

"Yes," Graser's voice whispered back from the other side of the hill. "The skeletons and zombies used deception when they build Redstone Castle and lured me out to explore it. I think it's fitting that we should use a little deception of our own."

"Oh, okay," said Brian, not sounding sure of things at all. "If you say so."

"I do!" insisted Graser. "Now get down there, and for goodness sake stop talking to me. The other skeletons will have seen you by now, they'll wonder what you're up to."

Graser was right. As Brian gathered his courage and looked back toward the zombie/skeleton construction project, he saw that the other undead were looking at him curiously, wondering what he was doing. Some of the construction workers even stopped their work to gawk. Brian quickly put on his brightest fake smile—skeletons were always smiling anyway, but he really gave it his best—and approached the massive building project.

"Hi everybody," Brian said when he was within earshot. "I've got some good news."

"Who are you?" one of the skeletons asked.

"You look familiar," said another skeleton who was hefting a block of chiseled quartz.

Then a senior-looking skeleton said, "Aren't you the one we left in the first room of the castle to administer Graser's first test. Don't tell me you've *abandoned your post*!?!?"

"No, no, no," Brian said, waving his bony hands to dismiss the idea. "Nothing like that. I came here because I've learned something that's really valuable for you to hear."

"Where's Graser, then?" the senior skeleton pressed.

"He's. . . he's. . . still trying to feed the Stone Wolf," Brian lied. "He's really bad at it too. He keeps feeding it all the wrong things. The Stone Wolf is getting really cranky about it, too."

"Heh heh, that's awesome," the senior skeleton said with an evil laugh.

"But here's the thing," Brian continued. "While he was dealing with the Stone Wolf, I heard Graser say something about his palace. He said there's a ring of lava around it that works like a booby trap to repel invaders."

"We already know *that*," snapped the senior skeleton. "What do you think we're building this bridge for?"

"There's more!" said Brian enthusiastically. "Graser said the lava moat is wide, but not very deep. He said that fools would spend their time trying to build a bridge over it. But that any smart person would just dig a tunnel *under* it. The lava is only about ten feet deep. A tunnel could go under the lava and lead right up to his palace door."

Skeleton faces are not expressive, but Brian could tell that the senior skeleton was evaluating this information carefully.

"And what would make Graser disclose such a thing?" the senior skeleton eventually asked.

"Oh," said Brian, thinking on his feet-bones. "He was talking about lava because he thought that the Stone Wolf would like to drink a milkshake made of lava. A lavashake! It was just one of the many things Graser got wrong! I know we made all these tricks to fool him in the castle, but I think we did more than we needed to. As it turns out, Graser's not all that clever."

"Hmm," said the senior skeleton, rubbing his jawbone with his hand, evidently deep in thought. Brian could tell he was making up his mind. The whole ploy hung on the edge of a knife.

"Yeah," the senior skeleton finally answered. "That sounds like Graser. He's not the sharpest tack in the box. I bet he would totally just blurt out the way through his defenses. Nice work!"

"Thanks," Brian said nervously.

The senior skeleton turned to the battalions of zombie and skeleton workers behind him.

"Okay folks," he said. "Change of plans. Drop all those crafting materials and pick up some pickaxes!"

As Brian watched dumbfounded, the zombies and skeletons obeyed their foreman. Instead of attempting to build a bridge over the lava, they started digging through the uppermost layers of dirt surrounding Graser's house.

"Hey you!" the senior skeleton said. "We're not paying you to stand around. You should pick up a shovel and help."

Of course, this made Brian very nervous because he knew what was about to happen. He glanced back to the edge of the hill where Graser and the ocelot were concealing themselves. Graser lifted his black metallic head out of cover for just a moment. One of his two red eyes flickered off and on. Brian realized this was a wink.

"Sure. . ." Brian said. "I'll be happy to help. No problem."

Brian took a pickaxe out of his inventory and joined the others.

The digging went very fast because there were so many zombies and skeletons. Their axes went up and down in a steady whir. Brian had once heard the axiom 'Many hands make light work.' Zombie and skeleton work was already usually on the lighter side (it just involved shooting arrows and attacking people, which was not too tough when you thought about it). This was just an extension of that saying.

When the hole in front of the lava was about twenty feet deep, the senior skeleton said: "All right, folks. Stop digging down, and start digging *across* toward the palace. We'll make our tunnel go underneath the lava flow."

The zombie and skeleton workers changed the direction of their digging and continued to hack away. Brian momentarily pulled himself back out of the pit and gazed once again in the direction of the hill where Graser and the ocelot concealed themselves. Brian looked and looked for any sign. He was very nervous. Then, finally, a black metal head popped over the horizon. It was accompanied by a metal handed that beckoned as if to say: 'Get the heck over here right quick!'

"What're *you* looking at?" the senior skeleton bellowed, noting that Brian was distracted. "Get back to work."

"Oh," said Brian. "I forgot something on the other side of that hill."

"What?" said the foreman.

"A. . . uh. . . very important thing," Brian said as he turned and began to race away as fast as him bony legs would carry him. "It's really, truly important. So important that I can't actually think of what to call it right now. But if you stay where you are, I promise to come right back with it and show it to you."

"Humph, fine!" said the senior skeleton with great annoyance. "But be quick about it!"

"Yessir," said Brian, but he was already too far away to be heard. Brian ran so fast he thought he might knock his bones out of joint. He was taking a tremendous risk and he knew it. But he also knew he owed it to Graser after what the crafter had done. Taking a big chance was the least that he could do.

Huffing and puffing with all his might, Brian eventually reached the hill where Graser and the ocelot were hiding. He dove over to the opposite side, landing in the grass with an undignified, bony thud.

"Ha!" the ocelot said. "You look like the skeleton in anatomy class when it falls off its hook and gets all jumbled up."

"When did *you* take anatomy class?" Brian asked, sorting himself out.

"What?" the ocelot said defensively. "I've been to ocelot school. It's harder than you think to be an ocelot."

An annoyed voice said: "Quite, both of you!"

The skeleton and ocelot fell silent.

Then Graser whispered in raspy tones: "It's about to happen."

Volcanoes were not a naturally occurring feature in most Minecraft landscapes. However, that didn't stop crafters from tinkering around and trying to build them. Even Graser himself had tried his hand at it a time or two. The trick was always getting the lava to flow across the mountain just right.

Graser knew that what the skeletons and zombies were doing was not going to result in a volcanic eruption. Not *exactly.* But Graser also knew it was going to be pretty darn close.

As Graser, Brian, and the ocelot watched, all the skeletons and zombies continued digging. All except for the boss skeleton who was looking around to see where Brian had gone. As his sockets scanned the horizon, they seemed to linger on the trio. The senior skeleton began to walk over.

"Darn it," said Graser. "He's seen us."

No sooner were the words out of Graser's mouth than it happened. The ground began to shake slightly, and there was the sound of liquid being sprayed. There was also the sound of lots *and lots* of zombies and skeletons crying out in surprise.

Brian just had time to ask: "What's that noise?"

As if to answer his question, an enormous spray of lava shot up out of the pit. It sprayed high into the sky, then fell back down and formed a sort of tidal wave. Graser had seen waves of lava before—even very big waves of lava—but he hadn't seen one with such a frothy foam before, and certainly not one that thrashed about so violently. His robotic eyes studied the churning lava carefully. It was soon clear to him that it was churning because it was full of zombies and skeletons who were none too happy about their current situation. They made the lava bubble like an angry, roiling boil.

Graser's lawn sloped downhill away from his palace. As he looked on, the lava began to carry the zombies and skeletons a safe distance away. It also demolished the bulwark they'd been building. So much lava had splashed so high that one side of the wall of Graser's palace was now coated with the shiny red stuff. Graser tried to feel annoyed by this, but couldn't. Considering the circumstances, it was a small price to pay. Besides, he thought to himself, the palace was probably due for a new paint job anyway.

"Omigosh, it actually worked!" Brian cried as the wave of lava swept past.

"Yippee!" said the ocelot. "How exciting!"

"Did we get all of them?" Brian asked.

Graser carefully surveyed the chaos on the other side of the hill.

"Well, it looks as though there's still one skeleton standing on a patch of dry land," Graser observed. "But I think you're wrong if you don't believe we got him. He looks pretty 'got' to me."

Brian and the ocelot followed Graser's glowing red gaze and found the senior skeleton supervisor. He had made it far enough away from the worksite to avoid being caught up in the initial lava explosion. Even though his bones were dry, he looked utterly defeated. It was obvious he could hardly believe what his empty eye sockets were showing him.

Graser emerged from the hill and walked out to meet the despondent skeleton.

On regarding the approaching black robot, the skeleton supervisor seemed shaken out of his stupor. He reached into his inventory and drew his bow.

Graser reached out and slapped the bow out of his fingers with a single motion.

"It's far too late for that," Graser said sternly. "What are you thinking? Don't you know I'm Graser. . .and you're just a single skeleton? I could make short work of you with one hand tied behind my back."

Graser had never seen a skeleton cry before, but the tremble in the skeleton's voice told him there could be a first time for everything.

"It's true, I am just a single skeleton now. A few moments ago I had a whole army. Boo hoo."

"A whole army that you were using to try to get inside my palace," Graser pointed out. "What a bunch of jerks. If you'd wanted to see inside, you could have asked. I do an open house every third Tuesday of the month. Of course, that's wasn't what you really wanted. To *see* inside."

The skeleton shook its head no.

"No, I admit it," said the gibbering skull. "We didn't want to just see all the awesome things inside of your palace. We wanted to take it for ourselves! To make it ours! I expect that seeing the inside would have just made us want it even more…"

"I realize you were envious, but you thought the solution was to trick me into leaving. . .and then march an army over to take my palace *by force*???" Graser asked sternly.

The skeleton shrugged.

"But you can craft things yourself!" Graser pointed out, his bafflement and frustration with the senior skeleton mounting.

"Huh?" it said.

"You crafted Redstone Castle yourself!" Graser said. "Why don't you just go live in that!?!? It had lots of cool stuff. It had a talking Stone Wolf, for goodness sake!"

"To be honest, we just found that," the senior skeleton admitted. "Someone else had crafted him already. We're really much better scavengers than we are crafters. You'll find that's typical with most skeletons. Anyhow, your palace is so much *cooler* than Redstone Castle. Even if we saw the inside and then tried to rebuild it block-by-block, it still wouldn't be the same thing. The fact that it was built by *you*—a famous crafter—really counts for a lot."

"So even if you had an identical palace to mine, I wouldn't be as cool because I didn't build it?" Graser said, a bit dumbfounded. "Is that really how things work?"

The senior skeleton merely nodded and shrugged.

Graser's bewilderment turned to frustration. His robotic eyebrows arched in anger.

"Just because you wanted a palace built by me, you tricked me into thinking that I had been contacted by whoever crafted me? You had to know that's one of the most personal areas of my life. You had to know it's something I'm really, *really* sensitive about!"

"Yes," said the senior skeleton. "We're sorry about that. But it was the only way we could be certain you would actually go to Redstone Castle. Any other mystery, you might have ignored. But not that one. Not you."

Graser's anger was growing. He gritted his mechanical teeth. He raised one arm menacingly.

The senior skeleton lifted a hand to shield his face and looked away. (If he'd had eyelids, he would have closed them tight!) The skeleton was ready to be smashed into a thousand bone-shards—or, at least, to be knocked into the lava flow and carried away with the rest of his compatriots. A tense moment passed. Then another. The skeleton braced for the worse.

But then when Graser's hand came, it was gentle. It rested on the skeleton's bony shoulder. It patted him reassuringly.

"I can't believe I'm saying this, but I'm going to help you," came Graser's voice. "If you're so envious that you feel you can't live—or whatever skeletons and zombies do—without a palace built by Graser, then we're going to get you one. But you're going to have to help. I'll show you guys the crafting tricks you'll need to know to build a grand palace. Then I'll even help you lay some of of the blocks so you can tell all your friends that you have an authentic 'Built by Graser' palace. How does that sound?"

The senior skeleton—who'd prepared to be bashed into oblivion just moments before, did not quite know what to say.

"Um. . . good," the senior skeleton managed. "That sounds really, really good. Thank you."

"Okay then," Graser responded. "It will take me some time to rebuild my own palace and repair the damage you have caused to my lava moat. Also, I expect it will take your troops quite a bit of time to collect themselves."

"I think you're right about that," the senior skeleton said. "We need to tend to our wounds for a while. I'll return later when we get things sorted out."

The senior skeleton turned and somberly walked away. Graser watched him go. As he did, Graser saw another figure walking in the opposite direction. This figure became familiar the closer and closer he got. Graser tried to place him. After a moment, Graser realized it was the old man whose cart had been stuck in the desert biome at the start of his journey. As the old man passed the skeleton going the other way, the old man didn't even flinch. He seemed very brave for an elderly villager, especially when confronted by a skeleton.

The old man saw Graser and waved. Graser, a bit surprised, waved back. Soon, the old man was close enough that they could speak.

"Quite a mess you have here," the old man said, surveying the lava and the remnants of the undead excavation work.

"You can say that again," Graser said to the man. "But don't worry. It's nothing a little crafting can't set right again. But say, what are you doing here? Shouldn't you be selling blue ice spikes somewhere?"

"Normally, yes," the old man said. "But today is a special occasion."

"Really?" said Graser. "How so?"

The old man leaned in closely.

"A wise man once told me that not everything in life that's a test *seems* to be a test at the time," the old man said. "but that doesn't mean its not still a test."

"Yes," Graser said. "In fact, I'm fond of quoting that exact same sentiment."

"Oh?" said the old man with a knowing smile. "Why? Have you also noticed that to be true?"

"I suppose that I. . ." Graser began, trying to remember.

"Or have you maybe *always* known it was true?" said the old man. "Almost as if you were born knowing. Or *built* knowing."

Graser hesitated.

"What are you saying?" Graser asked the man.

"I'm saying that I know the person who built you," the old man said. "Not like the skeletons and zombies. I *really* know who it was. And they wanted to meet you when the time was right. Seeing the kindness you showed me when my cart was broken, and all the other things you've done—oh yes, I was watching—I believe that the time is now right. Especially considering what you just offered the last standing skeleton. A lesser robot would have smacked him with a diamond sword. You instead said you would help him. That shows a level of clarity that few have. If you're ready, I can take you to meet the person who built you. Based on what you've done, I know they will be very proud of you."

Graser was so bewildered that he had to sit down.

"I just got back from a quest that I thought would let me meet my creator, and then I found out it was all a trick. Now you're telling me that it wasn't a trick? Or something?"

"A test within a test," the old man said with a gleam in his eye.

Graser stood back up.

"Fine," he said. "I'll come with you. But only if my new friends can come. Brian has redeemed himself as a skeleton and took a great risk to help protect my palace."

"Aww shucks," Brian said.

Graser continued: "And the ocelot has. . .let's call it a helpful point of view on things."

"I'll take it," said the ocelot with a grin.

"Of course your friends can come," the old man said. "The question is, are *you* ready?"

Graser thought about it for a moment.

He was.

"Yes," Graser told the old man. "You follow and I'll lead."

The old man smiled and turned. Graser and his friends followed after.

Graser didn't know who the old man was or where he would lead them—or even if this was truly how he would solve the mystery of who had built him—but he felt certain that his most exciting adventure might just be beginning.

THE END

Made in the USA
San Bernardino, CA
14 August 2018